MURDER IN

HUM

HARBOUR

Jayne E. Self

Dedication

To my amazing husband Harvey, to my friends who endured years of listening to my stories, and to The Word Guild which has supported, encouraged and taught me so much. Thank you.

Thanks also to Staff Sergeant Blair Bannerman for sharing his expertise on police matters; my editors, Tracey Fockler and Jamie West, for their guidance and expertise on writing; and Nicola Martinez, for all her work bringing my first novel to fruition.

Let all who have breath Praise the Lord!

Praise for Jayne E. Self

"[Jayne's] love of words and passion for the story are obvious in the way she writes."

~Cec Murphey, author of
NY Times Bestseller '90 Minutes in Heaven'

1

I learned something new about myself the day I found Doc Campbell. Dead bodies freak me out.

A cold fog shrouded the world that morning and after the weekend storm, the silent waves nuzzling the shore seemed insanely gentle. I kept my head down, studying the wet gravel as I walked. Anywhere, at any moment, a brilliant sliver of sea glass might catch my eye. Sea glass is a treasure to be gathered, hoarded and sparingly used in the jewelry I create. I spotted a slice of violet and crouched low, unable to believe my good fortune. Violet sea glass is among the rarest of jewels.

Beyond Hum Harbour's breakwater a foghorn sounded, its eerie echo raising the fine hairs on the back of my neck. A breeze whispered among the invisible evergreens on the hillside above me, and I looked up in time to see the fog shift ever so slightly.

I'd reached the end of the beach where ancient granite rocks guard the harbor mouth. They rise like a giant whale's back above the low tidal waters. Impaled on their slick black surface I saw the ghostly silhouette of a large boat. Stuffing the bit of violet glass into my gathering bag, I crept closer.

"Hello? Anybody there?"

The whole spooky scene seemed more fitting of a movie than my daily stroll along the beach, and my heart beat faster. Nothing seems alive on a foggy day. I usually find the sensation comforting, even cozy. But this morning it unnerved me.

"If you're there, please say something. I'm coming up to see if I can help." It might sound crazy warning a derelict cabin cruiser I was approaching but I didn't want any nasty surprises.

And surprised I was, because when I got close enough and read the name painted on the boat's hull, I knew whose boat this was.

"Doc? Are you in there?"

Doc Campbell is, or was, Hum Harbour's only doctor for the past thirty-some years. He'd just retired. In fact, his bon voyage party was Friday night, and he'd set off for the Caribbean at the crack of dawn the next morning. So what was his boat, the Medical Convention, doing here, on the rocks, on Monday?

Slipping, sliding, I scrambled up the rocks until I was above her and could see into the boat.

"Doc? Can you hear me?"

I tried to make sense of what lay before me. Wedged firmly on the rock, the Medical Convention listed badly to port. Several inches of water pooled in her lowest point, otherwise the deck looked neat as a pin. Crates were safely battened down, the tiny lifeboat securely fastened along the stern. The only sign of trouble, apart from the boat's obvious position on dry land, was the oddly-shaped lump propping the cruiser's cabin door open.

I leaned closer, then recoiled in shock. Doc Campbell lay face down in the pooled water, his pewter hair plastered against his skull, his broad shoulders motionless.

Heart in my throat, I ran.

2

"Slow down, Gai." My brother Andrew, one of Hum Harbour's three police officers, eyed me suspiciously as I crashed into the police station. "What is it this time?" He turned back to the box of donuts beside the coffee maker.

I waved towards the harbor and gasped for breath. "Doc's boat. I think he's dead."

Andrew's rust colored eyebrows furrowed as he bit into an apple fritter. "What are you talking about? Doc's probably in Maine by now."

"No, he's not. His boat's stuck on the rocks by the Murray place and he's lying on the deck. I don't think he's breathing."

Andrew studied me, trying to decide whether or not to ignore me.

I might be twenty-four but to Andrew I'd always be his irritating little sister and seldom worthy of serious consideration. "This is no joke, Andrew. Hurry up and get down there before the tide turns."

Rose McKenna, receptionist, secretary, radio dispatcher and all around office administrator, wagged her index finger in his direction. "Hop to it, MacDonald, or I'll let your little secret out of the bag."

My brother rolled his eyes and reached for his hat. Everyone in the family knew his secret. Andrew was studying French on the sly, hoping to make it into the Royal Canadian Mounted Police. He'd successfully passed the first level of interviews but flunked the French language requirement. So he'd hired a tutor in hopes of improving his performance. Time would tell.

"Don't forget that crime scene kit," said Rose, digging in the cupboard beside the photocopier. "You won't want to make an extra trip."

She pulled out a black suitcase. Its luggage tag read Crime Scene Kit in English and French, though why French I had no idea. No one in Hum Harbour, not even Andrew, spoke Canada's second official language.

Andrew grabbed a second donut instead.

"Come on," he said, pointing with his head. "We'll take the car, park in Ross Murray's drive and hike to the beach from there. You can show me exactly where to look."

Ross Murray lives in the palatial mansion at the end of the road. It's appallingly modern compared to everything else around Hum Harbour. The cop car crunched to a halt on the curving pebble drive and I jumped out of the passenger seat as soon as it stopped. Andrew disembarked more slowly.

Although no one emerged from the house as we rounded the garden, they'd know we'd been by. Our footprints left flat marks on their perfect lawn.

The fog blanket still covered the hillside. We took the stairs to the beach and turned left. In fifty meters or so we reached the rocks but we could see Doc's boat at about twenty-five. Andrew whistled.

"OK. So there's a boat." And when he climbed aboard he sighed. "And there's Doc."

I hugged myself tight, trying to hold in my shivers. In a way I'd been hoping I was wrong about Doc being dead. I liked him and had truly enjoyed the five years I'd worked as his medical receptionist.

Doc was handsome in a roguish sort of way, with a salty sense of humor and unkempt hair. True he liked to imbibe a bit—unfortunately, a lot of folks around here do—but Doc usually kept his drinking to the weekends when he sailed off on the Medical Convention for a little R&R. The liquor seldom affected his work.

Andrew hunkered down beside Doc and slid his fingers inside Doc's collar. He fumbled, as though he couldn't find a pulse and finally gave up. Pulling out his cell phone, he flipped it open with a flick of his wrist and keyed in the number with his thumb.

I held my breath as it rang through.

"Hey, Rose, we've got a situation. Get me some back up, and you might as well send the boys around."

'Send the boys' stopped my heart. Rose's family owned McKenna's Funeral Parlor. Any mention of the boys referred to Rose's two sons who did all their pick-ups.

I tugged at my hair. "Are you sure?"

"Yeah, I'm sure. He's been dead for at least twenty-four hours."

"How can you tell?"

"He's cold. Rigor's passed."

I scrubbed away tears with the back of my hand. "You should have listened to Rose and brought that suitcase. We could have started processing the crime scene before the others get here."

"That's not how it works, Gai. First on the scene secures the scene, makes notes and waits for back up and the coroner. Besides, what makes you think it's a crime?" He scanned the boat. "Looks like an accident to me. He was probably drunk, stumbled, and knocked his head on something."

"How do you know he was drunk?"

"When wasn't he drunk on the Convention? Besides, just take a deep breath." Standing on tiptoes, I leaned towards the boat and sniffed. "I can't smell anything."

"No? Well, I can, and he still smells like a distillery. Another sure sign he was pazooed."

"You shouldn't talk about him like that."

Andrew shook his head at me. "Get a life, Gai. You know as well as everyone else Doc retired early so he could dodge Sam's malpractice suit, which wouldn't be happening if Doc kept sober. And there's an empty twenty-sixer wedged under him. What more proof do you need?"

I wasn't impressed with Andrew's cavalier attitude. "Isn't there anything we can do?"

"Sure. You fetch the crime scene tape from the trunk of the car and I'll make notes like I'm supposed to."

"What kind of notes?"

"Time of day. Who called it in. What I see as first up." He pointed his pen. "Like that bottle, the rope holding the wheel in place. See?" Andrew indicated the taut length of cable that anchored the steering wheel to the pilot's chair.

"Is that what made him run aground?"

"Nah. Maybe. I dunno. More likely it just means he was down here in the cabin drinking instead of watching where he was going."

I studied the boat's deck too, trying to pick up the kind of details Andrew was looking for. "Is that an apple core?" I pointed at the brown mass floating in the pooled water in the deck's corner.

Andrew turned.

"And that, by the ladder. It looks like jewelry." Something silver was caught on the bottom rung of the ladder to the upper deck.

Andrew bent down. "How did you see that?"

"Professional training."

My brother snorted. He didn't consider jewelry making a profession.

He tapped the item with his pen and examined it. "It's an earring. Looks like the kinda stuff you make. You sure you didn't climb around in here before you fetched me?"

I stuck out my tongue. Fear of boats is an intolerable phobia when you grow up in a fishing village. It made me an easy target for teasing, which I usually ignored. "Throw me the car keys and I'll go get your tape."

I gladly scurried back up the hill. Staring at Doc's body made me queasy. No longer the dashing silver-haired gent who brightened my days, he looked like one of those inflated figures after the air had seeped out. As I rifled through the car trunk looking for Andrew's tape I almost apologized to God for such an irreverent thought. Then again, maybe that was the way He actually saw us.

I took my time on the beach stairs. Let Andrew scribble his notes. I was in no hurry to rejoin him. The fog was rolling back like window blinds and patches of brilliant blue sky would soon be visible. Already I could see the wharf, the fish plant and the cluster of old buildings that formed the village of Hum Harbour. The cross atop the church steeple appeared as I watched. May, like most months in Nova Scotia, enjoys versatile weather. That's one of the peculiarities of coastal living.

Commotion behind me interrupted my thoughts. Willie and Dale from McKenna's Funeral Parlor were trying to retract the stretcher's wheels before carting it down the wooden staircase. It was a comical routine worthy of a campfire skit, and I shuddered imagining them hauling Doc back up those same stairs.

Lord, please don't let them drop him!

I hurried the crime scene tape to Andrew, who ignored me and continued scribbling his notes. Meanwhile Willie and Dale dragged the stretcher along the beach.

Behind them trod the coroner, identified by the word 'coroner' plastered across his windbreaker in reflective lettering. Hum Harbour's new doctor took the rear. He, the new guy, gazed across the harbor as though he had all the time in the world, which I guess he did. I mean, Doc wasn't going anywhere.

"Why is he here?"

Andrew flashed me an inquisitive look. "Who? Grant? Helping the coroner, I guess. You gotta problem with that?"

I did. Geoff Grant's reappearance in Hum Harbour was as welcome as a cold sore. OK, not quite. He could come home and visit any time he wanted. It was the fact he'd moved back and taken over Doc's practice I objected to. To make matters worse he was now my boss. I didn't like taking orders from Geoff Grant any more than I liked taking them from my brothers, and I felt like a traitor every time I obeyed. I shook my head. "Why does the coroner need help?"

"Gimme a break, Gai, how should I know?" My brother flipped his note pad closed. "Look, I've got enough to keep track of here without you hassling me." He checked his watch. "Don't you need to be at work or something? What time does the clinic open?"

"Nine o'clock," I answered tartly, passing him the crime scene tape.

"Then hop to it or you're gonna be late."

He was right, of course. Monday's are an important day at the clinic. There are catch-up appointments, filing and billing, mail to sort. Geoff Grant brought a different work ethic, a different schedule and a whole different set of expectations to my job. At my age, I should be adaptable. It irked me that I found Geoff Grant and his changes so disturbing.

"Gailynn, good morning," Geoff said pleasantly.

I swallowed. Another thing I hated was the way my stomach reacted whenever he said my name. At any time the deep timbre of his voice turned my head, but when he said my name, well, my insides did this strange little flip thing which I'd yet to acceptably interpret. I fixed him with my best, blank face.

"I'd appreciate it if you could clear my appointments for the day. I've been invited to assist Dr. Brimmon with Doc Campbell's autopsy. He assures me it'll only take a couple of hours, but I think its best to clear my day, just in case."

"In case?"

"There can always be complications or delays."

Andrew nodded knowingly. "See, you can go now, Gailynn, we don't need you anymore. I'll get your statement this afternoon. Come by the station, will you? Save me tracking you down."

"Thanks." I glared at my brother. "If the clinic's quiet I'll be there around two." I spun on my heels and my ponytail whipped around like, well, a pony's tail. The effect was childish and I immediately regretted letting Andrew get under my skin. As I clambered off the rocks I heard Geoff Grant say, "I get the distinct impression your sister doesn't like me. Know why?"

"I expect it's got to do with Lori Fisher. Remember her?"

He groaned. "Oh, yeah, I remember Lori."

I wondered what exactly Geoff Grant meant by that.

3

I was in no condition to start work at a doctor's office. I still wore my grungy, smelly jeans and I was chilled to the bone, so I headed home. My cat, Sheba, greeted me enthusiastically as soon as I stepped inside the front door of Dunmaglass.

Dunmaglass is my shop. I used my first paycheck at Doc's as down payment on a neglected stone building on Hum Harbour's Main Street. It's about one hundred fifty years old, has two tall narrow stories with thick rock walls and a big window facing the street. I have the main floor set up as my shop, featuring my sea glass jewelry. I also display some stained glass panels and blown glass vases, both by local artisans. I truly believe Dunmaglass will be famous someday, but until then I'll keep working at the clinic. After all, a girl's got to eat.

My apartment is above the shop. When I'm at work, Sheba prowls the two floors. She's my guard cat, twenty-three pounds of pure black sinew. She has a white star on her forehead that reminds me of an exotic gem, hence the name Sheba, after the queen. Most mornings Sheba joins me on my seashore hikes. Today something in the air suggested she stay home.

I walked across the shop while she twined through my legs.

"Wish I'd listened to you," I told her. "Maybe Doc

would still be alive." That, of course, was ridiculous. But if I still thought Doc was alive didn't that make it almost the same?

I scooped Sheba into my arms and buried my face in her warm fur. Tears burned my eyes.

"Lord, you know how much I hate when things change. Couldn't you have stopped this?" I talk to God out loud when I'm home alone. Unfortunately, He never answers in kind.

Instead, Sheba wriggled free and raced for the stairs. God's way of reminding me I didn't control the world any more than I controlled my cat, I guess.

She meowed.

"I'm coming," I muttered, following her up the steep steps.

She pawed open the kitchen cupboard. Sheba chose which can she wanted and I opened it. That was our agreement. As she ate and my coffee brewed, I had a very long, shower. When the hot water and my tear ducts eventually ran out, I toweled dry, donned my uniform and headed to Doc Campbell's, scratch that, Doctor Grant's office.

I had graduated from high school with no life goal apart from never wanting to leave home, which is hardly an admirable ambition in this day and age. So when my best friend Lori Fisher's mom suggested I consider taking over her job at Doc Campbell's office, I thought, "why not?" and signed up for a ten-month course at the local college. In no time I became a certified medical receptionist.

When I started my course, I didn't realize Lori's mom had been diagnosed with cancer. She always seemed so healthy and full of life I imagined she was simply prodding me into the kind of low-pressure career I could handle. Not that Ellen Fisher was any slouch. Quite the opposite. I knew Lori got her brains, and her love of medicine, from her Mom. I think Ellen would have been a doctor if she'd had the opportunity. Tragically, she passed away this past winter, not living long enough to see Lori settled in Doc Campbell's medical practice—which didn't happen, anyway. Instead, just when we all thought Lori would step into the good Doc's shoes, he went and sold the practice to Geoffrey Burton Grant, of all people.

****

Doc's office is on Blair Street. It's a single-story shake cottage, your typical Nova Scotia kind of house with an add-on veranda to shelter the front door from the worst of the weather and give people a place to kick the snow off their boots in winter. Mounting the steps, I collected the mail from the box marked Douglas Campbell MD and unlocked the front door.

I stepped inside and switched on the lights. I'd done this same thing five mornings a week for the last five years, yet suddenly the routine felt foreign.

I scanned the waiting room as if seeing it for the first time. In a way, it was the first time, at least the first time without the possibility of Doc Campbell striding into the room with his joke of the day. Most of his jokes were awful, but kids loved them. Nothing calmed and distracted a sick kid more than a lousy joke. Their moms loved Doc for it.

I hung up my coat and booted up the computer. As it hummed to life, I sifted through the mail, absently flipping the junk flyers into the recycling bin, slicing open the bills and assorted correspondence. I still sorted them into piles the way Doc liked them, not bothered that Geoff Grant preferred things done differently. The computer screen blinked on, and I opened the day's appointment schedule.

This morning was our Well Baby Clinic. That meant new moms bringing their progeny to be weighed, measured and immunized as necessary. I knew all four moms scheduled and called each to rebook for Friday afternoon.

Doc routinely took Friday afternoons off, but Geoff Grant wouldn't know that, and I felt pretty confident he was not a closet drinker desperate for the weekend. Geoff Grant was back in Canada after serving five years with International Medical Missions in a Muslim area of Somalia. Not much opportunity for him to bend the elbow there.

The office door creaked open and Lori Fisher poked her head in.

"Is he here?"

I waved our 'coast is clear' sign and Lori stepped inside. She perched on the corner of my desk and surveyed the office that was supposed to be hers, not Geoff Grant's. Her honey blonde hair cascaded through the back of her ball cap. Lori's beautiful, with violet-blue eyes, skin like a California beach girl, and a figure to die for. She turns the head of every man she's ever met. And she's smart. Lori'd just passed her final exams and was licensed to practice Family Medicine in Nova Scotia. We all assumed she'd move home and work with Doc. Then, in a few years time Lori would take over his practice. Instead, two weeks ago Doc announced his early retirement and the sale of his practice to former Hum Harbour resident, Dr. Geoffrey Grant.

"I just heard," she said. "What does Andrew think happened?" Whenever Lori mentions my brother the cop her perfectly shaped brows rise ever so slightly. She's been in love with Andrew since elementary school. My brother, however, seems immune to her charms. He just applies and re-applies for the RCMP, as though becoming a Mountie is the only thing that will satisfy his heart. I sometimes wonder why Lori doesn't give up on him, but I guess you don't make it through medical school if you're the kind of girl who caves whenever your goals seem difficult to reach.

I leaned back in my chair. "He said it was probably an accident. Doc had this big bump on his head." Pressing my fist against my left temple, I demonstrated. "The wind must have pushed the Medical Convention back into the harbor after Doc was knocked unconscious."

She wrinkled her nose. "Yuck. Do you think he died instantly? I hope he did. It would be awful to lie there alone and die slowly, don't you think?"

I pictured Doc as I'd seen him Friday night: handsome, jovial and drunk. The thought he might have lain for hours turned my stomach. My fingers wrapped around the silver cross I wore and I said a silent prayer. "I guess that's the kind of thing Geoff and the coroner will figure out when they do the autopsy," I said.

Lori reached for the antiseptic moisturizing hand cream on my desk. "Geoff, is it?" The edge in her voice pricked me.

"Well, I can hardly call him Doc, can I? And he said Doctor Grant sounded too formal. In Somalia they called him Doctor Geoff."

She concentrated on massaging the cream into her

scuffed knuckles. "Doctor Geoff? You're kidding, right?"

"No, Doctor Lori, I'm not. I suppose it might work here if he was a pediatrician but since he's not, I figure I'm stuck with calling him Geoff."

"So why is Geoff doing the autopsy? Doesn't the county coroner do that?"

"Apparently he invited Geoff to assist him. Maybe it's some kind of medical bonding ritual. After what Geoff told us at church we know he's big into bonding."

Two Sundays ago, our pastor invited Geoff Grant to share stories about his experiences in Africa during morning worship. By happenstance, as Reverend Innes introduced Geoff he also mentioned Geoff would be staying in Hum Harbour indefinitely because he'd just bought Doc Campbell's medical practice. Whether or not that was the way Doc intended the news to get out, it was out. And once something is announced from the pulpit at Third Church everyone knows it's as true as the sky is blue.

I confess, I did not take the announcement well.

While everyone else in the congregation listened in spellbound silence to Geoff talk about the beauty of the African people he worked with, the open hearts of the kids, the infectious joy of even the most impoverished, all I could think about was Lori. And how for years we'd planned when we'd work together at the Hum Harbour clinic. And now, in the blink of an eye, that dream was kaput, squashed, destroyed. Annihilated.

Sitting in my pew, my heart pounded. My mouth went stone dry. I erupted from my seat in a most inappropriate fashion and, like a madman in a C-grade movie, pointed my shaking finger at Geoff shouting,

"How dare you prance back into Hum Harbour and ruin people's lives, Geoffrey Grant." To make matters even worse, I furiously stamped my foot, twice. "What right do you have to steal our dreams?"

I think his mouth dropped open, but I couldn't say for sure because, most humiliating of all, I promptly burst into tears and fled the church.

When you think about it, it really was quite extraordinary that two weeks later I was calling him Geoff as if we'd been pals for years.

Lori held out her hand. "So Geoff's gone all morning?"

"All day, in fact." I fished around in my desk drawer and came out with a small bandage. "Here. Look, I've got billing stuff to finish. Wanna meet later? I don't think there'd be a problem if I took an extended lunch and we treated ourselves at the Hubris Heron."

Lori's eyes twinkled teasingly. "We could do take-out and eat on the boat. I'm still going to be sanding old paint off the Lori-Girl in August—if my hands survive, that is." She wrapped the bandage around the scuffed knuckle on her right index finger. "If you came to me I could work another half hour today." Lori was spending the summer fixing up her dad's old lobster boat. He had visions of offering harbor tours to tourists.

"If you are so concerned about your productivity why are you dawdling here?"

She slid off the desk. "I just needed to know if it was true. Poor Doc. All he wanted to do was see the Caribbean. Why couldn't God let him have that one last wish?"

I had no idea. But by nightfall, I'd learn that God had nothing to do with cutting Doc's retirement short.

4

I was late for my lunch with Lori. I trotted down the middle of Blair Street, my steps getting faster as the slope grew steeper. Everywhere I looked, there were colors bursting to life.

I love the month of May. Tulips, daffodils, birch and aspen trees shiver yellow green in the wind. I think every yard in Hum Harbour has at least three lilac bushes and when they're in bloom, the entire hillside is awash in shades of violet—my favorite color. And the fragrance…

This morning, lilac blossoms were only a week or two away.

Hum Harbour is a snug little cove opening onto Saint Georges Bay. Dark, forested hills plunge towards the rocky shoreline that sits like a ring along the water's edge. When the tide is out you can walk all the way around the cove on the gravel beach. When the tide's in, only a narrow strip is accessible.

The village of Hum Harbour hugs the inner most curve of the cove. Its four major streets run parallel to the shore, each one riding higher along the slope of the hill. Water Street skirts the harbor. You access the wharf, the fish plant, and Hum Harbour Bait and Tackle from Water Street.

Above Water is Main Street, the business section of town. Besides Dunmaglass and the Hubris Heron

Seafood Café, there's the drug store, post office, dry cleaners, Hum Harbour Hardware, and Hunter's Monument and Toys.

McKenna's Funeral Home is the only business on Pictou Street, unless you consider Third Church a business. I've attended Third Church all my life, as have most everyone in Hum Harbour. People passing through town assume the church's name refers to the Trinity. In fact, it does not. Hum Harbour's First Church burned down in 1875 and its replacement, Second Church, met a similar end in 1922, hence Third Church. Some people think is overdue for replacement, too. Naturally, I am not one of them.

Murray Street is uppermost and it connects to the highway.

Mimi Johnson is owner-operator of Hum Harbour's number one eating establishment, the Hubris Heron Seafood Cafe. She's a bit of a character, which I say with the greatest love since she's my dad's first cousin once removed. She's stout, in a healthy Scottish sort of way, with hazel eyes and ultra-curly auburn hair. Besides being a wife, mother, and restaurant owner, she's our local naturopath. Not that she has an official license or anything, she's just committed to holistic remedies and has developed a successful business selling them.

She has a gorgeous kitchen garden next door to the café and untold rows of echinacea and roses growing up the hill behind her house.

When I reached the café, Hugo, the six-foot wooden heron who presides over the front door, regarded me disdainfully. The last time I'd visited the Heron was for Doc's retirement-bon voyage bash three nights before. How things change.

That night Hugo wore a humungous yellow bow with a dozen helium-filled balloons bobbing and bumping his beak. A gigantic Good Luck Doc sign filled the café window and all 363 residents of Hum Harbour crammed themselves into the tiny restaurant. Or so it seemed.

To say I had mixed feelings about Doc's departure wouldn't do justice to my conflicting emotions, but, at the time, I attributed the twisting knot in my stomach to sadness. Despite that, I wanted the night to be perfect for Doc. I wanted him to know how much we loved him. I wanted him to realize no matter how his Caribbean retirement faired, he'd always be welcome in Hum Harbour.

The Heron was decorated with rainbow streamers and oversized floral bouquets. The LeBlancs played their fiddles, and Mimi did herself proud with a spread most Halifax caterers would have charged a fortune for. There were chocolate brownies, oatcakes, fruit tarts, matrimonial squares and these incredible little lavender custards. Plenty of veggies and yogurt dip, too, but I preferred the sweets. The centerpiece was Mimi's famous coconut cream pie. Golden meringue flecked with toasted coconut curls and shimmering beads of liquid sugar, it sat atop her grandmother's cranberry glass cake plate commanding everyone's eye. We all knew it was Doc's favorite, and only he was allowed to eat it.

As I worked my way through the crowd, making sure everyone was happily fed and watered, I listened to the chatter. I discovered not all wished Doc a smooth send off.

Particularly Ross Murray, Mike Johnson and Bud Fisher. The three stood beside the dessert counter, their voices rising above the clamor. I elbowed my way towards them, hoping something simple like an empty dessert plate caused their distress. I was wrong.

"He can't do this," Bud said. "He signed an agreement."

Bud is Lori's dad and owns Hum Harbour Bait and Tackle. He's had a hard time since Ellen died. Coupled with the recent closure of the fish plant and reduction in business, he's had a lot of empty hours on his hands. He's been filling them with drink.

"It's only binding if he's dead, Bud." Mike, Mimi's husband and owner of Hum Harbour Hardware, popped half an oatcake into his mouth.

"What do you mean by that?"

"We all signed it," Mike said. "Didn't you read the fine print?"

My ears pricked.

"What fine print?"

"Come on, Bud, how did you keep your business going all these years? Ellen do all your paperwork?"

"What if she did?"

Ross Murray, whose belly overhung his belt buckle more than Bud's ball cap overshadowed his nose, selected the largest brownie in sight. "Well, Bud, if she did," he said, skimming off the icing and licking his finger, "she probably would've noticed the little clause allowing any of us to back out of the project within six months of our original signing date. It's called an escape clause."

Their voices slipped back into the normal range, forcing me to press closer if I still wanted to listen. I did.

"This ain't six months."

"Sure is," said Mike. "It was six months on the nail

when Doc told us he was taking his money to the Caribbean with him. I bet he's already put it in one of those Grand Cayman accounts you hear about in the movies."

"Grand Cayman accounts?" Bud's words slurred, a sure sign there was more than fruit punch in his cup.

"They're inaccessible to the taxman, like Swiss bank accounts," said Ross. He'd recently sold Murray Enterprises to some German conglomerate. Protecting his taxable income would undoubtedly be a big concern these days.

Mike looked worried. "What's going to happen to Hum Harbour Holes? Without Doc's quarter mil, can we still go ahead?"

Hum Harbour Holes was the brainchild of Doc, Ross, Mike and Bud. With the closure of the fish plant and, dare I say, the impending job layoffs at Murray's Sawmill, Hum Harbour's economy was less than stellar. And as with most small towns in Nova Scotia, people were looking for ways to bring in the tourist buck. Pictou has the HMS Hector, Antigonish its Highland Games. We will have a golf course.

Ross scratched his head. "Well, I've got my accountant working on that very thing, but I've got to tell you, Mike, I think it's going to be tight. We're already running behind schedule according to the income projections. We may need to dig a little deeper to make this go."

"Deeper? How deep do you expect us to reach? Not all of us have made our fortune off the Germans."

"Yeah," muttered Bud. "Not all of us have bottomless pockets."

At that point, Doc Campbell had joined them. I hoped he'd lay their concerns to rest. "What are you three on about?" he asked, munching the last bit of coconut cream pie on his plate.

"We're discussing the Holes," said Ross. "Trying to figure a way around the mess you've created."

Doc pointed his fork towards Geoff Grant, who stood half a head above most other people in the room. Geoff happened to be chatting with Reverend Innes.

"See that man there?" Doc said. "He's the future of this town. Hit him up. Offer him a free life membership to buy in."

Bud snorted contemptuously. "He's a missionary. Where's he gonna get a quarter million dollars?"

"He had no trouble anteing up to buy my practice."

Bud drained his cup. "Maybe you and him made some kinda deal to make up for what you did to his sister. That lawsuit of hers could ruin you."

Doc licked his fork. "You're drunk."

"And you ain't?"

"Cut it out you two and keep your voices down," shouted Mike. He was louder than Doc and Bud combined.

I grabbed a plate of chocolate brownies and shoved it between them. "Squares anyone?"

Ross took two.

"That all you can suggest? Offer Grant a free life membership?"

"He's a doctor isn't he?"

"How about another slice of pie?" I asked, prying Doc's empty plate from his hand. I refilled it, whether he wanted the second piece or not.

"You made a commitment. You can't just waltz out of Hum Harbour as if nothing matters," Mike said.

Doc shrugged, and the way Bud's face twisted I

thought he might take a swing at him.

Ross grabbed Bud's arm before I could react.

"Doc obviously doesn't care a twit what happens to us and our money," Ross said. "But a missionary and a golf course? That's plain stupid. The guy'd probably want to shut the place on Sundays. No way to run a business."

Bud and Mike grunted, and I wondered if Geoff Grant was as narrow minded as they thought. I mean missionaries are known for their God-focus, and Geoff did start every clinic day with prayer.

From his spot against the far wall, Geoff glanced up. His gaze found mine and he nodded.

I swallowed.

"We need a way to guarantee the money," Mike said. "Hum Harbour Holes is too important to let die."

But Doc was already threading his way through the crowd, apparently dismissing Hum Harbour Holes and his former partners from his mind. I still held his pie.

"Got any idea how to do that?" I asked Mike.

He, Ross and Bud Fisher turned slowly to me. "Gailynn," they said, raising their glasses in unison. Their pointedly blank expressions left me uncertain.

"My Lori Girl's lookin' for you," said Bud.

"Yeah, Mimi's trying to get your attention," said Mike.

I could see neither.

"Whatever you come up with, don't you dare ruin Doc's party," I warned. "Tonight's important, too."

All three tapped their foreheads with the traditional scout's honor salute. "We won't," they promised.

Believing them honest, trustworthy men, I left

them discussing how they might save their golf course, and I sailed after Doc with his second slice of pie.

Now, three days later as I pushed open the Hubris Heron's blue door, I reflected on the unnerving tension I'd experienced Friday night, realizing it wasn't sadness. It was apprehension.

5

The Hubris Heron's décor is largely defined by its space. Since the old stone building is long and narrow there are cozy booths against the north wall, tables down the middle and the counter along the other side. The booths and tables are portable—hence the sardine crowd of Friday night—the counter is not.

Mimi has a loyal clientele. I noted the regulars as I poured two mugs of coffee, one for me and one for Lori. I plunked our drinks on the one vacant table and sank into my chair.

Reverend Innes inclined his head in greeting, too busy wolfing down Mimi's daily special to say hello. Conversations wafted around me. I expected the usual mix of weather, politics and fishing, but today everyone was talking about Doc. I should have known.

"Hey, Gailynn, I heard you found the old geezer." That was from my oldest brother, Sam, who has no tact. He runs Dad's fishing boat now that Dad's retired. He makes a pretty good living.

Sam and his wife, Sasha, bought a big century home on the hill, planning to fill it with kids. After ten years of marriage, they're still childless. I love Sasha like a sister and her heartbreak is my heartbreak.

I glared at Sam over the rim of my mug. "Doc is not a geezer. Don't you have any respect for the dead?"

Reverend Innes, his mouth full of Mimi's

succulent biscuit, nodded.

Sam ignored us both. "I thought he'd live forever. You know, permanently pickled?"

"Give the girl a break," said Mike. He sat across from Sam, which meant I couldn't see him.

Everyone loves Mike. He's a man's man, the original tool guy. He drives a souped-up pick-up that every male in town drools over, if my brothers are any indication, and he tends to disappear for days at a time. No one knows why, but since it doesn't appear to stress Mimi, it doesn't stress me, although I do wonder how he runs a successful hardware store that way.

"I heard her hull'd been ripped wide open," Mike said. "She'd a sunk to the bottom if she hadn't been tossed on the rocks."

"I heard he'd been shot by some of them dope dealers who keep smuggling stuff in from South America." Bud Fisher slid a metal flask from his jacket pocket and, when Reverend Innes wasn't looking, liberally poured its contents into his coffee. No one commented.

Lori knocked on the front window before stepping inside.

Her dad grinned proudly—he did that whenever Lori was near—and shouted his usual greeting. "Hey, Lori Girl."

She heyed him back and settled into the chair opposite me. Flipping her hair free from her cap, she tossed the hat toward the coat hook. It landed perfectly and she winked at her dad.

"I taught her everything she knows," Bud said. Bud said that every time Lori threw a ringer, which was every time she tossed her hat.

I returned to the subject we'd been discussing.

"Doc was not shot. Andrew thinks it was an accident."

"Andrew ought to know," Reverend Innes said.

Bud sipped his coffee. "Bad luck for you, MacDonald. How're you gonna get paid for that lawsuit you started?" He elbowed Sam in the ribs.

Sam didn't seem to notice the poke. "I dunno. Maybe his estate'll still cover that sort of thing. Or his insurance. Didn't you tell me, Gailynn, Doc paid malpractice insurance?"

I considered socking him. I felt guilty enough about Sam and Sasha's lawsuit as it was. Sam broadcasting my involvement felt like coals of shame heaped on my head. "I would never tell you anything that personal about Doc's business. I only might have said all doctors pay malpractice insurance."

"Yeah, well, close enough."

Bud snagged a biscuit from the basket on the table. "You're gonna have to stand in line, MacDonald. Mike and me claim first dibs on any money the Doc left. Ain't that right, Mike?"

"Eh?"

"The Holes," said Bud. "Maybe it can still go ahead. This town sure needs it."

"I dunno. Maybe Doc pulling out like that was a sign a golf course in Hum Harbour's a bad idea," said Sam.

"Yeah? Then why did God strike him dead for turnin' his back on his friends?"

"God did not strike Doc dead. It was an accident. Don't you listen?" I demanded.

Sam looked at Reverend Innes. "Since when did accidents stop being a sign of God's providence?"

"Since forever," I answered on the reverend's behalf.

My brother grunted. "I'm only repeatin' what I hear other people say."

Lori stirred sugar into her coffee. She now had two bandage-wrapped fingers. "Sam MacDonald, you're worse than an old woman."

Mimi bustled out of the kitchen carrying bowls of steaming chowder. "Why don't you fellas be quiet and eat your lunch?" she said, setting the soup on our table.

"Otherwise, I'm going to give the last two slices of my key lime pie to these girls."

Sam immediately began mopping his plate with his biscuit. Beside him, Bud did the same. Reverend Innes, who'd spent more time eating than talking, held out his empty plate.

Mike grabbed Mimi's apron ties, reeling her in. "Ah, honey, you know the last piece is always for me."

"Yes I do." She smiled sweetly and slipped out of his grip. Ignoring the mile high pie under the glass dome on the counter, she retrieved an especially succulent looking slice from the cooler and presented it to Mike. She winked at Reverend Innes. "I'll get you a piece in a moment, Reverend."

I wasn't interested in pie. All this talk about lawsuits and Hum Harbour Holes made me uncomfortably aware of how fortuitous Doc's accidental death was. I needed a dessert-free brain so I could think. I had serious questions about whether Doc's demise had been an accident at all.

6

My afternoon interview with my brother the cop proved brief. Rose McKenna had already filled out the report's identifying information; all she needed to add was my driver's license number. Then I dictated my statement to Andrew. He wanted facts, none of the mood stuff, like the creepy sense of foreboding in the pit of my stomach when I awoke this morning, or the way the hairs on the back of my neck quivered when the mist parted and I first spied the Medical Convention marooned on the rocks.

Despite the apparent speed of the process, it was close to four before I closed the police station door and started home.

Although Andrew insisted I was overreacting, my thoughts kept going back to Friday night when Ross, Mike, and Bud shooed me away so they could talk in private. According to what I'd already overheard, Doc's investment in Hum Harbour Holes would've been guaranteed if he died before fulfilling his financial commitment. The estate would cover his quarter million. Did that still apply if Doc had already activated his escape clause and backed out of the deal?

To me it sounded logical that Doc's estate would be off the hook, but logic was never my strong suit—ask either of my brothers. Who could I ask about this?

My first choice, Dad, was away with Mom. They'd

flown to Vancouver Island for Mom's cousin's daughter's wedding. My brothers, Sam and Andrew, would never stoop to answer even if I asked them, and I could hardly go to Mimi. She knew as much about contracts and escape clauses as she knew about recipes and plants, but how do you say, "Excuse me, is your husband capable of murder if the price is right?" and not get the door slammed in your face? Same with Lori. How could I trouble her, especially considering how worried she was about her dad?

There was the lawyer who did the paperwork when I bought Dunmaglass, but he charged minimum twenty bucks for every phone call and seventy-five for an office visit. How badly did I want my question answered?

That's as far as I'd thought when Geoff Grant caught up with me.

Geoff left Hum Harbour when I was thirteen and apart from a few brief sightings when he visited during university holidays, I'd not seen him until three weeks ago. While in Africa he mailed home the odd black and white photos his sister posted on the church bulletin board—a vaguely familiar white man lost among dozens of dark-faced kids. He looked very different in color.

His light brown hair, no longer buzzed to oblivion, was just long enough to seem permanently disheveled by the wind. His features were still sharp. Mom said he needed fattening but I found his square jaw and strong nose rather attractive. And when he smiled at me, which he was doing, the crevice-like lines in his cheeks dimpled flirtatiously. Geoff's eyes were striking. They were deep set, heavily lashed and the blue-green of glacial ice lit from within.

This morning, he'd wrapped a wooly scarf, which just happened to be the exact same blue as his eyes, around his neck and turned up the collar of his winter jacket. He looked half frozen and intolerably handsome. I tried to ignore my stomach's response.

As a doctor, Geoff would surely understand the intricacies of the law and he had no personal stake in Doc's death. He was just the man I wanted to see. I gave him my friendliest smile.

"How did your interview go?" he asked, his smile widening.

"I don't think you could technically call it an interview," I said and picked up the pace lest he think I was staring.

"OK, how did your not-technically-an-interview go?"

"Fine. Andrew has no imagination."

He nodded in apparent agreement. "I doubt imagination's a highly prized commodity in police circles. Do you want me to talk to him about something?"

"Not Andrew, no. I need you to answer a question for me, though."

With the afternoon wind blowing off the water and snatching away our words he leaned closer. "Fire away."

I sucked in my breath. "Hypothetically speaking," I began, "what if a certain person, well several certain persons, signed a document agreeing to contribute financially to a certain project and one of those certain people changed their mind and cancelled their part in that agreement. Would that person's estate still be obligated to fulfill their agreement once that certain person died, especially if that certain person died under questionable circumstances?"

He pinched the bridge of his nose. "I see why you don't want to ask your brother."

"But can you answer my question?"

"I'm not even sure what your question is."

So I started again. "If certain people signed a certain document that said they all agreed to pay X number of dollars— "

Geoff pulled me against his chest.

For a split second I was totally, mindlessly, blissfully, engulfed in his wonderful scent. Kind of like sinking into the bottomless ocean, but not nearly as terrifying. Then Billy Johnson flashed by and Geoff set me aside. Billy constantly rides his skateboard down Hum Harbour's steepest hills at near-death speeds. Distracted by Geoff Grant's company and my muddled thoughts, I'd forgotten how dangerous Hum Harbour could be.

Geoff led me to the edge of the road and checked me for bruises. Of course, there were none, but I liked the way concern deepened the clefts in his cheeks, so I encourage him to take his time.

"I assume you were referring to Hum Harbour Holes," he said, bringing me back to the subject at hand.

"You know about the golf course?"

"Gailynn, everyone in town knows about it and has three opinions apiece."

"What's that supposed to mean?"

He shrugged. "Just a comment on life in Hum Harbour. Are you asking me if Doc died under questionable circumstances? Or are you asking if his estate still has to pay what he agreed to pay?"

"Do they have to pay?"

"I have no idea."

Why not? I almost shouted. His handsome edge had worn off, and I no longer felt breathless, just annoyed. "It can't be that complicated. Either the document is binding or it's not."

"Why don't you ask someone else who signed the document?"

My jaw dropped. "Because what if they killed Doc to guarantee his money?"

It was Geoff's turn to do the jaw drop. "You're kidding, right?"

"I heard Mike, Ross and Bud at Doc's retirement party and they were trying to come up with a plan to make sure Doc honored his investment in the Holes."

"And now you think the three of them put their heads together and decided murder was a plausible solution." He said it as though I was out of my tree.

"You tell me. Was Doc murdered?"

"Is that what this is about?" He stuffed fists into his coat pockets, looking equally annoyed, although I couldn't see why he should be. "You want to know what the coroner found during the autopsy."

"No I don't. Well, yes I do want to know, but that's not what this is all about."

He studied me, his annoyance apparently replaced by curiosity. "You seriously think one of these men whom you've known all your life is capable of murder?"

Put that way, the answer was no, so I dodged his question. "Does that mean the coroner proved Doc was murdered?"

"He hasn't proven anything."

I chewed the inside of my cheek. "Then he hasn't proven Doc's death was natural causes, either?"

"It may be natural causes if Doc died of a heart attack or stroke, depending on what caused his heart attack or stroke."

"But you don't know?"

"Not yet."

We fell back into step as I thought that through. "If the bump on his head caused his fatal heart attack or stroke, then it's not natural?"

Geoff had his hand on my elbow, guiding me. Perhaps he thought Billy would return. "No. That's death by misadventure."

"And if someone caused Doc to fall and get bashed in the head?"

"If that were the case, and if Andrew and the police could prove it, that would be murder."

"A lot of if's."

He nodded. "A lot of if's."

"What if you were the one who signed a paper guaranteeing you'd pay Ross and his crew a quarter million dollars and you changed your mind and then you turned up dead a couple days later? Wouldn't you think that was suspicious? Or want others to think it was?"

"Of course I would. But I'd want the police asking questions, not you."

"What's so wrong with me?" I pushed his hand away. This was so typical. No one thought I could figure my way out of a wet paper bag, let alone put two and two together and get four.

Rising on tiptoes, I looked him straight in the eyes. "I would be every bit as capable of solving your murder as my brother the cop." I poked his broad chest for effect. "Just because I don't understand contracts like the one Doc and the guys signed does not mean I don't understand human nature. I've lived in this town my whole life and I know every single person who lives here. I know their strengths and I know their weaknesses, and just because I'm related to half of them does not mean I'm incapable of seeing their flaws."

He held up his hands. "Whoa."

But I was on a roll. "I'll tell you what I think. I think there's something fishy going on and Doc's death was too convenient to be natural causes. I think one of those men, or all of them, figured they were going to make sure Doc paid his part of the golf course just like he promised. And I think they did something. I don't know what they did but they did something that made Doc have that heart attack or stroke. And while the coroner is dragging his heels trying to figure out what it was they did that made Doc die, I'm going to figure out who it was!"

He took a few moments to answer. "I don't think that's a good idea."

"Who asked you?"

"You did when you asked me if I thought Doc's contract was binding." He gently took my fisted hands off my hips and held them until I calmed. "If, and I say if with a great deal of reservation, *if* one or all three of those men were involved in a conspiracy to kill Doc Campbell, they are not the kind of people you think they are. They're dangerous. And dangerous men, when threatened with exposure, do bad things to the people who threaten them."

I rolled my eyes. "I'm not stupid."

"But you're innocent. You've lived your entire life in a town where people are kind and polite and treat each other with respect. You have no idea what dangerous people are capable of."

"You can't have it both ways. Which is Hum Harbour? Paradise or Sin City?"

"I guess that depends on whether you're right or wrong about Doc's death."

I shivered. "So you can't answer my question about Doc's contract?"

He released me. "Nope. Have you checked the office? Maybe he left a copy in the clinic's files."

"I never thought of that."

"Well I give you permission to go through every file you can find. Take your time. Just promise me one thing."

"What's that?"

"If you find anything, you'll show it to me, and if it's relevant we'll take it to Andrew together."

I dug my toe into the ground and considered his proposal. I could always sneak back to the clinic at night and go through Doc's files without Geoff's permission, but if I did, and found something, who could I approach about it? Without Geoff's consent, I had no right to snoop through the drawers full of files. I might even get charged with breach of privacy or something. No, it was better to keep Geoff in the loop. I mean, later on I could always ignore his advice if I didn't like it. He was only asking me to consult with him. He wasn't telling me what I could or could not do. Yet.

I held out my hand. "Agreed."

7

"In the mean time, could I ask a favor?"

Geoff still held my hand, and the way he looked at me I think I might have agreed to anything—which was ridiculous because I'm not that kind of girl. I do not get twitter-pated and tongue-tied around men. I'm more the kind to punch them on the shoulder and spit in their eye. At least that's what my brothers say, and since I've never been romantically linked with anyone, I've been inclined to accept their assessment of me.

"A favor?" I repeated.

"I've some notes I need downloaded on my computer and with all that's happened today, I won't be able to get around to them. Could I presume upon you to transcribe them onto my laptop for me? I know it's a lot to ask, but I promised to do some special music at church on Sunday and I'm supposed to meet with Edna Sinclair tonight. It's the only night she's free." Edna was Third Church's organist.

We'd reached Main Street and turned left, stopping in front of Dunmaglass.

"You want them put on your laptop, you say?"

He nodded, his eyes twinkling. He knew I coveted his jazzy little notebook and was dying to get my hands on it. OK, dying was a bad choice of word.

"You OK?"

I guess my face must have fallen. I sighed. Was it

only this morning I found Doc's body? Only today I started doubting the people around me? I felt as though a hundred pounds of fish bait hung on my back.

"I'm fine," I said unconvincingly.

Maybe Geoff's request was a godsend. The more technical and boring his notes the more I'd have to apply myself to the task. In fact, now that I thought about it, I rather liked the idea of concentrating on something other than Doc's death. "Sure, I'd be happy to do that up for you."

"Shall I drop my computer off when I head to the church at seven?"

"Why not just pass it across the rail when you get upstairs?" I suggested instead. Geoff lived next door in the apartment above the Hubris Heron.

Both of our places have a back terrace. Mine is cozy, filled with wicker chairs and big potted plants in summer, Christmas stuff in winter. Geoff's is empty except for whatever the wind blows in. It's also larger than mine because it extends over the Hubris Heron's kitchen, a definite plus since his apartment is hot and cramped. Geoff apparently prefers an apartment to the lovely bungalows Sasha had shown him—I think I already mentioned Geoff's sister Sasha also happens to be my sister-in-law?

Until Geoff moved in, Mimi filled the vacant apartment with a century's worth of empty shipping boxes. Geoff paid her kids a nickel a box to flatten and bind the unwanted cardboard, and I heard they bought a new video game system with their proceeds.

I have never been inside Geoff's apartment, but Sasha tells me it was in bad shape. Parts of the ceiling had fallen in; the plaster was mildewed and there was serious evidence that squirrels once lived in the kitchen cupboard. I could never imagine wanting such a dive but Geoff seemed convinced he could fix it up and make it livable. I guess you don't go into missionary work if you're the kind of person who's overly concerned with luxury. Anyway, Mimi's husband, Mike, donates any building supplies Geoff needs and Mimi's reportedly cut Geoff's rent in half.

All this to explain how I could walk upstairs to my own home, open the sliding door that leads to my deck and find Geoff Grant leaning against the terrace railing, laptop in hand.

At the sight of Geoff, Sheba shot out of my arms and landed on the rail. Purring louder than the trawler puffing back to the wharf, she rubbed wantonly against him.

He ruffled her ears. "Hey, girl, I have a treat for you."

Sheba pranced to the open tin of tuna awaiting her. Tucking in her paws daintily, I assume that's when she says grace, she then gobbled Geoff's offering.

"Have you ever seen a panther kitten?" Geoff asked. "They're about Sheba's size."

I untied my ponytail and let the wind lift my hair. "Can't say I've seen too many panthers running around town, no."

He laughed and handed me an unlabeled folder containing his notes. "It was a little disconcerting to move home and find a wild cat living next door."

"As long as you're referring to Sheba I won't take offense."

Geoff tilted his chin. "I'm not sure. Your eyes are the same color as a lion's, you know."

I delivered my best lion growl and Geoff laughed

again.

Suddenly feeling self-conscious, I opened the folder and scanned the heading at the top of the first page. Autopsy: Douglas James Campbell. Doc. My fingers went numb.

"You should've told me what this was about."

"Would you rather not do this for me?" He held out his hand.

I jumped out of reach, hugging the folder close to my chest. "No, I'll do this. I want to do this. You just should have warned me. Are you allowed to have this information?"

"I was there, Gailynn. I can hardly pretend I saw nothing. And these are not official notes. They're simply my observations recorded for my own records."

"And that's allowed?" I hungrily scanned the five pages of scribble. What I really wanted to ask was am *I* allowed? I mean, here, in my hot little hands, were all the details Geoff had noted during the coroner's autopsy. Maybe the very clue to how Doc died. Geoff was crazy if he thought I'd back out now.

"May I have your computer?"

He passed it over. "Can you read my writing?"

"I'll manage. Why not stop by when you're done at the church. I should be finished."

Geoff agreed and I carried his laptop inside.

****

I'm not the most meticulous housekeeper in the world. I collected my jewelry tools, clearing a spot on what was once my grandmother's table. While I prepared supper, I read through Geoff's notes. His handwriting was decipherable and where he used medical terms like hematemesis he'd gone back later and printed the word in upper case letters. So once I'd eaten, I pulled out the medical dictionary Lori had given me when I first started at Doc's office, and typed Geoff's unofficial autopsy report into his computer.

It took longer than I expected because I had a hard time keeping my thoughts on track. The notes would say peri-mortem hematoma and I'd picture the goose egg on the side of Doc's head and I'd rewind my imagination to the moment I first spotted his lifeless body. Aspirated water translated to Doc face down on the deck, which led me to wonder about that apple core I'd spotted. Stomach contents sent to the provincial lab for toxicological analysis: how much alcohol had Doc consumed? And where were all the empties?

Was the Medical Convention still tied up with crime scene tape? How many cops did it take to process a crime scene? Did they even consider the Convention a crime scene? Andrew certainly held reservations. He was convinced Doc's death was accidental. Death by misadventure, Geoff called it.

I hit spell check.

Misadventure, my foot. Instead of sitting here typing up Geoff's boring, conclusion-less observations I should have been rummaging through Doc's files looking for a copy of the Hum Harbour Holes contract. I'd learn a whole lot more from Doc's documents than a hundred pages of this autopsy mumbo-jumbo.

I wanted to slap myself. How dumb could I be? Geoff knew very well his notes would tell me nothing. He'd used them to distract me from my commitment to find Doc's killer. The information in this autopsy was irrelevant and now I'd wasted half my evening.

I checked my watch. There was still time. I pushed save and darted downstairs. Stuffing myself into coat and shoes, I was half way to the door when the buzzer rang. Geoff. Groan.

Normally everyone in Hum Harbour leaves their doors unlocked, and if you're dropping by you just stick your head inside and holler. However, since I moved over Dunmaglass I keep my door locked. The stained glass panels and blown glass vases in the shop were worth a small fortune. I'd hate for anything to happen to them.

Andrew, not Geoff, cupped his hands against the shop's front window and peered inside. "Let me in, will you?" he shouted as soon as I flicked on the overhead lights.

I unlocked the door and Sheba dashed by, almost knocking Andrew off balance. He still wore his uniform.

"I'm on my way out."

Andrew flashed his badge. "Police business. We need to talk."

"Can't it wait 'til morning?"

Andrew elbowed his way inside. "Won't take long. Shall we go upstairs?"

When Andrew got a bee in his bonnet there was no distracting him. Resigning myself to the delay, I swept my arm towards the back stairs.

"After you, officer."

He shook his head. "You first. I don't want anyone claiming I made an unlawful entry."

Rolling my eyes, I mounted the steps.

Sheba already waited at the top.

"Would you like some tea? Or is that not allowed when you're on official business?"

Out of the corner of my eye I saw Andrew walk over to my table, flip through Geoff's notes, study the computer.

"What's all this?"

"Geoff asked me to enter his notes from Doc's autopsy. Apparently he likes to keep his own records in case there are questions."

He humphed. "Stopped by his apartment, wanted to talk to him about what they found, but he wasn't home. Maybe you can explain this to me." He lifted the folder.

The bell above the shop door jingled, saving me from answering.

"Hello? You up there, Gailynn?"

I glared at my brother. "Now look what you let me do. The door's unlocked. Anyone could have slipped in and snatched something." I handed Andrew his tea and hurried downstairs again, welcoming Geoff Grant into the premises. Sheba twined between his legs. I relocked the door and invited Geoff upstairs, too. It was the first time he'd been inside my establishment. I saw him glance around the shop before scooping Sheba into his arms and ascending the stairs.

"Hey," he greeted Andrew. And noting my brother's uniform, "I guess it's been a long day for you."

"Don't have many accidental deaths in Hum Harbour. RCMP are letting me take part in the investigation. Big opportunity. Came by to ask Gailynn a couple extra questions I should have covered in her statement."

"You didn't tell me that when you came in."

"Didn't I? Guess I got distracted. Gailynn tells me she's doin' up Doc's autopsy report for you."

"Just notes for myself."

I passed Geoff a mug of tea with milk. "I'm done. You can look it over now while Andrew interrogates me."

"It's not an interrogation, Gai. Just a couple more questions."

"Then question away. I have nothing to hide."

Andrew dug in his pocket and pulled out his notepad. "Tell me again, did you step aboard the Medical Convention to confirm Doc's condition?"

A ridiculous question, my brother knew very well I would never set foot on any boat, afloat or aground. "I did not."

"Did you reach in or toss anything onboard?"

"Does handing you the Crime Scene tape count?"

"I'm interested in anything you might have done when you were alone with Doc's boat before you called for the police."

"Then no, I did not touch or contaminate the scene in any way. I watch TV too, Andrew. I know better than to mess with a crime scene."

"You keep saying crime scene."

"Admit it. The RCMP think Doc's death was suspicious."

Ignoring the gibe, Andrew showed me a tiny zip-lock baggie. Inside was the silver earring he found on the deck of the Medical Convention.

My breath caught in my throat for a moment. "It's one of mine." I said what he already knew.

"Yours personally or one of your creations you've sold?"

Geoff left the computer and stood behind me. Reaching over my shoulder he took the earring and held it up to the light. The violet seaglass glowed.

"I'd need to check my files, to know for sure. If I sold it I'll have a record."

"Then go," Andrew said impatiently. "I'll wait."

I escaped to the shop for my receipts, my mind frantic. I knew the earring well, but did I want to admit it? If I told Andrew who the earring belonged to he'd be out my door in a flash and I could still do some sleuthing of my own tonight. On the other hand, he'd immediately be banging down someone else's door. I didn't relish that.

I dumped my drawer of receipts into a shoebox.

There would be a perfectly innocent reason for the earring being on the Medical Convention. Its owner just needed a heads up, a chance to remember the details without Andrew breathing down her throat.

Then again, maybe if she experienced Andrew in full cop mode, she'd see for herself how committed he was to his RCMP dream, and finally realize they simply weren't suited for each other. If the earring even belonged to Lori.

You see, here was my problem. The earring Andrew found on Doc's boat was one of three matched sets I made as gifts to my two closest friends, Lori Fisher and Sasha MacDonald. We all had a pair. Now, Lori might have logical reason for being on Doc's boat to wish him good-bye but Sasha? She and Sam were suing Doc for malpractice and I couldn't see how anything good could come out of Andrew demanding answers from Sasha at this time of night.

Sasha was having personal problems and, let me put it this way, no one would ever convict my brother Andrew of tact. It was a trait my brothers shared.

I took the shoebox full of receipts back upstairs and plunked it in the middle of the coffee table.

Settling myself on the couch, I withdrew a handful of them. I could see Andrew's eyes widen.

"These are my receipts from the first four months of this year. I'll have to go through my filing cabinet for ones from Christmas and before that."

He groaned. "Didn't know you were selling this much stuff."

A sore spot with me was how my two older brothers laughed at my craft. They thought making jewelry from bits of seaglass was a kid's hobby. Nothing worthy of an adult's time, certainly not an adult's dollar.

"I do. And someday I'll make a good living at it too." I plucked out one receipt and waved it under his nose. "See this? One set of deep blue earrings and matching necklace, sterling silver settings, one-fifty."

"One-fifty? That's it?"

"That's one-hundred, Andrew, not one dollar. If the settings were gold it would be three hundred and fifty dollars."

He snatched the paper out of my hand to see for himself that I wasn't pulling his leg.

"People pay that much?" He nabbed another receipt out of the box. "These earrings were only twenty-five dollars."

"They're green glass. That's the most common and the easiest to match. The rarer the glass, the harder to make a matched set, the more costly the pair."

"So blue is rarer than green?"

"And red is rarer than blue."

He looked at the violet earring in his tiny bag and I prayed he would not ask how common violet glass was because it was the least common of all. He'd realize I was fishing for time, that I knew exactly where every piece of violet glass jewelry I'd made had ended up.

"Where did you find that earring?" Geoff asked Andrew, saving me from Andrew's next inevitable question.

"Medical Convention."

I busied myself sorting through the sales slips. "Are you thinking there was a woman on Doc's boat? I suppose it's possible he entertained women on the weekends when he sailed out of town."

"Women who owned your jewelry?"

"Well, I really couldn't say."

"Could you say if Doc bought the earrings and gave them to some woman as a gift?"

I spread my hands. "Andrew, if you want me to go through all these bills of sale to find one for this particular earring it could take all night. Do you need it immediately?"

"No. Just want to have all the loose ends accounted for. Don't want someone coming back to me later saying I did a slip-shod job on this investigation. Want this to look good on my resume."

"Ah, the RCMP."

"You bet. I want them to see I am Mountie material all the way."

Geoff sighed. "Then maybe, Andrew, you'll want to have a closer look at what we found during Doc's autopsy. I'm not convinced Doc's death was an accident."

8

"Not an accident?" repeated Andrew.

"You understand this is only my opinion and not the official findings of the coroner."

"Will his findings confirm your opinion?" Andrew asked.

Geoff nodded. "I believe they will but it'll take time. According to the coroner, the provincial lab is overworked and understaffed. It'll take days, maybe weeks, before they get to the samples he sent today."

"Does Andrew have to wait for those results before he can investigate?" I asked Geoff.

Andrew stuffed the earring bag back into his pocket. "Don't intend to sit on my hands and let evidence slip through my fingers," he said. "What have you got for me?"

"As you remember, when we initially examined Doc the coroner said the contusion on Doc's head may have rendered him unconscious, but it wasn't fatal. It was possible that Doc aspirated some of the sea water on the deck, in which case, his official C.O.D., uh, cause of death," he explained, no doubt for my benefit, "would be drowning. Whether or not we found fluid in his bronchi or lungs would confirm our hypothesis."

"And?" Andrew and I said in unison.

"I believe Doc's stomach contents may lead us to another conclusion."

Andrew flipped open his note pad expectantly. "I'm standin' here with bated breath, Geoff. What did you find?"

"Questions."

"What kind of questions?"

"There was blood in Doc's stomach. We sent samples of stomach contents for toxicology but who knows when they'll have their analysis completed."

"Doc probably had an ulcer. No surprise there, he was a weekend alcoholic," said Andrew.

"Except I don't think the bleeding was a result of an ulcer."

"What do you mean?"

"Do you want a technical analysis of the condition of his stomach lining or the shorter layman's version?"

"Shorter'll do."

"Long term bleeding from an ulcer leaves a variety of signs, depending on where the ulcer is located, its size and of course, how long the patient suffered from the ulcer. An ulcer is a fairly localized phenomenon. The patient might have more than one ulcer but the entire lining of his stomach or duodenum—that's the small intestines—isn't affected. You with me so far?"

Andrew nodded. "This is the short version?"

"You need to know about ulcers to understand why I'm concerned about the frank, uh, fresh blood in Doc's stomach. You see, although Doc's stomach indicates a history of ulcers—there were several scars and a current blossoming ulceration he was no doubt taking medication for—his entire stomach lining was damaged."

"So?"

"Something damaged it."

"Can you be a little more specific?"

"Unfortunately, no, not until those lab results come back."

"Ah, come on. You must have some idea, otherwise you wouldn't have mentioned it. What do you think? Cancer? New strain of the stomach flu? Ebola? Gimme a hint, a guess even."

"Poison."

Andrew sank onto the couch. "Poison? Who would want to poison Doc?"

"I don't know, but I think your job is to find out."

"What kind of poison?"

"I don't know that, either. Maybe the lab will be able to isolate it."

"Maybe?"

"Hopefully? Look, Andrew, the lab screens for whatever it's asked to screen for. There is no all inclusive lab test that can identify every poison known to man. They can check for obvious poisons like cyanide, strychnine—"

"Alcohol," I inserted. "Maybe he just drank too much too fast."

"Unlikely for an alcoholic. His tolerance level would be much higher than yours or mine, and unless Andrew found a dozen empties hidden somewhere on board?"

"Nope. Only one empty twenty-sixer stuck underneath him."

"Then he didn't drink himself to death."

"Had he eaten anything?"

"There was a fruit and cheese basket in the cabin. Looked like some of the cheese had been eaten," said Andrew.

"And grapes, judging from stomach contents."

"A fruit basket?" I guess that explained the apple

core.

"Someone probably gave it to him as a bon-voyage present."

"What if they poisoned the stuff in the basket?" I suggested.

"Again, that depends on what they identify at the lab."

Andrew pushed himself to his feet. "Guess I better get that basket sent in, too."

"Not a bad idea."

"Ever had to do anything like this in Africa?"

"Only once. Usually the deaths I dealt with were pretty straightforward. TB, malaria, AIDS."

"What was the one time?" I couldn't help asking.

"A woman murdered her rival using poison made from Cinchona bark. Horrible way to die."

"You think someone poisoned Doc with this Cinchona bark?" The possibility sounded far-fetched to me.

"No, it just reminded me of the case, raised a couple of red flags for me."

****

By the time Geoff and Andrew left it was pouring rain and I had no desire to search Doc's files. Instead, I crawled into bed.

My bedroom faces Main Street. The Victorian style lamp posts that lit Main flooded my room with their brooding glow and I left my curtains open. Rain pelted the windowpane. Writhing purple shadows twisted across my walls and ceiling. A block away, the sea roared louder than a thousand herds of Geoff's African lions. I dragged the blankets up to my chin.

I'd promised Andrew I'd find the earring's bill of sale by tomorrow. It didn't exist, though, and now I had to come up with a believable excuse for stonewalling my brother.

Part of the challenge of making seaglass jewelry was finding pieces with the same shape. I know some people manufacture seaglass artificially. They cut colored glass into whatever shape they want and polish it in a stone tumbler. Or they anchor mesh bags full of glass in the surf. But my glass is completely natural and any matching is by God's grace, straight and simple.

Over the years, I had unearthed six identical crescents of violet glass. I crafted those six pieces into the earrings that Sasha, Lori and I now owned. Before tucking myself into bed, I checked my jewelry case. My set was safe.

First thing in the morning, before I told my brother, I would visit both friends and discretely inquire about theirs.

****

Naturally, things didn't work the way I intended.

Andrew's police cruiser was outside Dunmaglass when I came downstairs next morning. I was earlier than usual because I planned to pop in at Lori's on my way to the clinic. Seeing Andrew leaning against the car door sipping his morning cup of take-out coffee, I considered ducking out the back. However, when he smiled and waved, I could hardly turn and run.

I fiddled with the door while I composed my face.

"You're up early," he said. "Big day ahead?"

"Nothing special," I answered. "And you? You don't usually drop by this early."

"As I recall, last night you promised to find me a

bill of sale for those earrings." He held out his hand. "I've come to collect."

Andrew's empty hand waited.

"I wasn't completely honest with you last night," I said, bracing myself. "I never really technically sold the earrings."

"They were stolen?"

"I, uh, gave them away."

He shrugged. "That'll make them simple enough to trace. Who'd you give them to?"

"Two people, actually, three if you count my pair. I made them as friendship gifts. I have one set. Lori has the second pair and Sasha has the third."

Andrew pushed back his hat and scratched his head. "Where's yours?"

I thought the silver and violet crescents dangling from my ears would have been more obvious. "Are you sure you're ready for the RCMP?"

Andrew turned my chin, giving himself a better view of my earrings. "OK, you have yours. I'll check out Sasha and Lori."

"Why don't you let me talk to them? I mean, I could find what you want to know a lot more discreetly than you could."

"Gailynn, this is an official police investigation. I don't need to be discreet."

"But these are our friends. Family. You do need to be sensitive. Sasha's been so miserable lately. I won't have you barging in accusing her of who only knows what."

"Bet Doc's demise perked her up. Kind of like God's doing payback on her behalf, don't you think?"

I glared at my brother. "God does not do payback, Andrew."

His right hand swept into the air as though raising an imaginary sword in battle. "Remember our Sunday school lessons? Vengeance is mine, sayeth the Lord."

Marjorie Murray, our old Sunday school teacher, came instantly to mind. I could still see her standing on the chair in the church basement, brandishing her cardboard flaming sword. I might not remember the lesson, but that image had a big impact and Andrew often delighted in rekindling the memory.

He sheathed his pretend sword. "Stay out of it, Gailynn. Don't interfere with my witnesses."

I tugged at my hair. "I have a right to talk to my friends."

"Don't have the right to interfere in a police investigation, though. I could charge you with obstruction of justice."

I held up my hands. "Fine. Talk to Sasha. See for yourself she has nothing to do with Doc's death. But, if you make her cry, Andrew, so help me I will be all over you like the rot on Fisher's lobster boat."

"Speaking of which, maybe I'll head over to Fisher's and talk to Lori first. She won't cry if I ask her anything."

I reached for the car door. "I'll come with you."

"Not a chance, little sister." He grasped my shoulders and spun me around. "Go to Doc's clinic and do your job while I do mine."

My composure snapped. I hadn't slept well and I'd already drank three cups of coffee to combat the weariness. "Stop pushing me around," I said and punched him hard. "And it's not Doc's clinic anymore."

Andrew's brows pulled together as he considered me. He absently rubbed his chest. "Thought you liked

Geoff."

"Well I don't. I wish he stayed in Africa where he belonged. Doc would still be alive if he hadn't come home and messed everything up."

"You can't be serious?"

"Why not?" I wasn't, but that didn't stop me suggesting it. If Andrew could go after my friends, I was going after his.

He stood with fists on his hips. "Give me one good reason why Geoff Grant would bump off Doc."

I couldn't, and Andrew knew it. "Fine, but you haven't got any reason for suspecting Sasha and Lori either."

"Who says they're suspects? Gailynn, I am just trying to trace an earring. That's it. End of story. So, get off your high horse, and like I said before, go to work."

I gasped when I checked my watch: three minutes to nine. Arguing with Andrew cost me my chance to warn my friends. "Now I'm late for work," I said. "Satisfied?"

"Oh yeah, I live to interfere in your life. The goal of my day." Andrew climbed back into his car, slamming the door so hard the windows rattled, and drove off in a puff of exhaust.

I hiked my bag onto my shoulder and ran.

9

Chicken pox was on the loose in Hum Harbour and business at the clinic was hectic. I had a headache by the time I locked the door for lunch at two-thirty, an hour and a half later than usual. I nabbed some pain killers from the medicine cabinet and popped my salad out of the fridge.

By now, Andrew had talked to Lori and Sasha. How did it go? I tried to imagine why either of my friends might board the Medical Convention.

Lori's mom had worked for Doc since before Lori was born. Growing up, Lori went to my house or the clinic every day after school. That was thirteen years worth of after-schools spent at the clinic. Lori knew Doc well. It would be perfectly reasonable for Lori to stop by the Medical Convention. And perhaps her earring got knocked off when she hugged him good-bye. Yes, that was how her earring ended up on Doc's boat.

It was Lori's earring, and there was no sinister mystery about how it got there.

I didn't entertain the possibility the earring might be Sasha's. Too many complications, too many problems, if Sasha was onboard Doc's boat. No, I told myself emphatically, there was no need to explore the bad blood between Sasha and Doc, because Sasha wasn't involved.

But what if I was wrong? Jabbing my salad with my fork made me think of Andrew poking Sasha with his insensitive questions. Would she be OK? Maybe I should drop by the shop and check, just to be sure. I mean, it's not like I'd miss anything exciting if I dumped my lunch. So I did.

"Back in a minute," I shouted to Geoff and high tailed it out the door before Andrew's warning to stay out of things made me re-think my visit.

Sasha worked at McKenna's Flowers, which was attached to McKenna's Funeral Home. Some think a florist and funeral home are an odd combination but I think it's a rather smart move on the McKennas' part. I mean, where do you see flower arrangements most often? I suppose some brides might consider purchasing their wedding bouquets from a mortuary a bad omen but, hey, this is the twenty-first century.

That Tuesday afternoon I found my sister-in-law alone in the shop. She looked paler than usual and the dark smudges under her eyes made them seen as large and as deep as the sea.

I hugged her tight. Despite the thick fairisle sweater she wore, Sasha felt bonier than a lobster trap. "Can we talk?" I asked.

"Come into the back with me while I make up this basket."

I followed Sasha into the room behind the glass flower cooler. I loved sneaking back here because I love the blend of fragrances, roses, carnations, gardenias. A luxurious gift basket of imported chocolate and something satiny sat ready for delivery. Sasha pulled a ceramic dish from the shelf and began filling it with the different plants waiting on her worktable. I watched her hands. They trembled ever so slightly.

"Has Andrew been by, by any chance?"

"Oh, were you looking for him?" She tried to sound casual but she wasn't fooling me.

"Apparently he found one of our violet earrings on the Medical Convention and he's trying to figure out which one of us it belongs to."

"Why would it matter?"

"He's probably trying to find the last person to see Doc alive."

"Well I already told him it couldn't have been me."

"He was here, then?"

Sasha surveyed her work and nervously twiddled her silver earring. She did that when she was unhappy. Lately it seemed she did it all the time. Things were not running smoothly between Sasha and my brother Sam.

She removed two of the plants. "Doc's dead. It's unfortunate, but I don't see what I have to do with it."

"You and Sam are, or were, suing Doc for malpractice. Maybe Andrew thought you talked to him one last time."

"Well I didn't. What would be the point? It's not like talking could undo what happened to me."

"I know and I'm sorry. Whenever I think about what happened I feel so responsible."

"How are you responsible for me losing our baby?"

"If I hadn't called Doc back that day, if I'd just minded my own business and let you go into Emergency in Antigonish, another doctor would've looked after you. You would've had better care."

Sasha was tiny, with a slender heart shaped face that always looked sad. At that moment, the misery in her face almost broke my heart. "Sam wasn't there to help me know what to do, so I asked you to call Doc, remember? I insisted. If it's anyone's fault it's mine."

"But you didn't know how drunk Doc was."

"Did you?"

"Well, no, but it was a Friday afternoon. I should have guessed."

"Look, Gailynn, it's over. There is no going back, so why go on about it?"

She sounded so weary. Because I insisted on calling Doc, and he mucked up her treatment when he did arrive, she lost the baby she and Sam had tried so hard to conceive. The small fortune they'd spent on that fertility clinic in Halifax was gone, leaving them with no savings for a second try. But instead of blaming those of us responsible for her loss, like me, Sasha turned her grief back on herself. She was drowning in despair and there seemed to be nothing I could do to help her.

Miserable, I changed the subject. "So you told Andrew you weren't on the boat?"

Sasha reworked the arrangement she was creating. "I couldn't lie." She dug into the dirt with her fingertips, wedging an African violet into place. "Ross Murray ordered a basket delivered to the Medical Convention. He knew Doc said no retirement gifts but he wanted Doc to have something as a bon voyage. So I made that up and delivered it Friday afternoon."

"Andrew asked if you were wearing your violet earrings?"

"I can't remember what earrings I put in this morning let alone what I wore five days ago." Her voice slid higher.

"As long as you can produce both earrings it really

won't matter."

"What if I can't? Andrew gave me until tonight to find them. He said if I can't show him my earrings by then, he could get a search warrant and go through our whole house." Sasha sounded close to tears. "He can't go through our house, Gailynn."

I hugged her again. "Don't you worry. You'll find those earrings at home where they belong. I promise."

"What if I borrow yours? I could show him yours and say they were mine and he would go away and leave me alone."

I pulled back. She wouldn't lie to Andrew but she was OK with tricking him? "I don't think that's a good idea."

"He won't know." She looked hopeful, maybe even desperate. "And it'd be just for tonight. I'll give them back tomorrow, once Andrew sees them."

"I don't think its right. What if he found out and charged us with something."

"How would he find out? I'd never tell."

I stuffed my hands deep into my pockets. "I think you should look for yours before we start plotting."

"But if I can't find mine, will you help me, Gailynn?"

The shop's doorbell rang and I jumped. It felt like God had sounded a warning buzzer from heaven.

"Please?" Sasha said again.

"Sasha, you back there?" I recognized Vi Murray's voice. She could be very persistent.

"You better go and see what Vi wants," I told Sasha. "And I have to get back to work. We'll talk later."

My stomach in knots, I escaped the flower shop and ran back to the clinic. *Lord, what am I going to do now?*

I couldn't lie. The very thought made my stomach clench in panic.

It was just Sasha's depression talking. She wasn't thinking clearly, that's why she'd suggested it. My earrings were close at hand while hers were somewhere in her house and it would take more effort to hunt them down than she had energy for. But if she didn't hunt them down, Andrew threatened to come looking with a search warrant. Imagine what a mess he'd make, snooping through every nook and cranny of Sasha's big old house. And then she'd have to put everything back when he was done. Sam wouldn't help. It would never enter his fat head to lift a hand around the house and help Sasha.

Lie? I shook my head. I might avoid the truth, but I worked very hard to never openly lie.

Though it wasn't as if Sasha was guilty of anything. If anyone was guilty it was me. I mean, Sasha's depression was really my fault. Sure she said it wasn't, but that was friendship talking, not truth. If Sasha was willing to turn a blind eye to my part in her miscarriage, shouldn't I be willing to make sacrifices, too? Was it really lying to let Sasha borrow my earrings?

"Are you planning to stand there all day?"

Geoff's question snapped me out of my thoughts and I found myself in the clinic's open doorway, hanging onto the doorknob as if it were some kind of lifeline.

I blinked a couple of times and pried my fingers loose. "Thinking."

"Must be important."

I stepped inside and shut the door. Afternoon

clinic hours would begin soon. Already one mom and toddler occupied the waiting room.

"I stopped by McKenna's to see Sasha," I said. "I guess Andrew'd been by this morning."

"How's she doing?" Geoff asked in a hushed voice.

With the racket her daughter was making, I doubt the Mom could hear us, anyway.

I wasn't sure what to tell Sasha's brother about our conversation. "I'm worried. Andrew thinks she'll probably snap out of her depression now that Doc's gone but..." I hesitated. "I think she's worse. Could you talk to her?"

Geoff propped his hip against the corner of my desk. "Believe me, I've tried but she and Sam have built such a wall around themselves. They're hurt and angry, and I understand, but until they're ready to let someone in, there's not much I can do."

I frowned. Geoff sounded content to sit back and wait. Maybe he was right. Maybe that was the wisest thing to do and I should wait, too. But when have I ever been wise?

Before I had opportunity to ponder that bit of self-recrimination, the little girl in the waiting room threw up all over her mother. From that point on my afternoon was filled with seemingly more urgent concerns.

After the last patient went home, Geoff and I stacked the waiting room furniture in the back room. The janitor had to shampoo the carpets overnight. Cramming plastic chairs against the bank of filing cabinets, I remembered Geoff's suggestion I check Doc's files for his copy of the Hum Harbour Holes Agreement. Last night I was busy transcribing Geoff's version of Doc's autopsy report. Tonight, obviously, would not be the night, either. That was OK with me because I had other plans.

10

Sometime during the afternoon, I'd made a decision. I couldn't tell Geoff about Sasha's suggestion we lie about her earrings; that would breach her trust, but I could act on it. Once I was done with work, I waved good-bye to Geoff and trotted to my cousin, Mimi's place.

Mimi would have something among her stock of medicinal herbs to combat Sasha's depression. And if it came in tea form, I was sure Sasha would drink it without questioning its hidden benefits.

As I pushed open the white picket gate, Mimi's dogs barked from her garden. They raced towards me between the rows of bright green clumps of new growth. April rains might bring May flowers in the rest of the world, but in Nova Scotia, May plants are mostly unidentifiable globs of promise. At least to me.

Mimi followed her dogs. She wore muddy jeans, one of Mike's plaid work shirts and orange plastic garden clogs. Her three dachshunds, Oscar, Meyer and Frank, beat her down the hill and threw themselves at my ankles, tummies up.

I hunkered down and rubbed them.

Mimi wiped her hands on her shirttail. "What brings you here?" she asked after we hugged.

"I'm looking for professional help."

Her eyebrows disappeared under her auburn

bangs.

"For Sasha."

"Ah." She led me inside her plant room without further ado.

Just as I'm not sure about Mimi's official title, I'm never sure what to call her room. An apothecary? A drying room? A workshop? An office? It has shelves full of labeled bottles, racks suspended from the ceiling which, at various times of year, overflow with bundles of dead plants. An old steel office desk is pushed into one corner. No computer, just a manual typewriter and a Rolodex. In the centre of the room, her wooden worktable, an ancient butcher-block, is marred from years of use. At the moment, it held two mortar and pestles of different sizes. The larger bowl contained lavender, which I knew from the scent. The smaller held something hard and black like peppercorns.

"The S's had a row last night," she said, meaning Sam and Sasha. My brother and his wife lived directly downhill from Mike and Mimi, the M's. "I had the bedroom window open and they woke me up."

"What was wrong?"

"I've gotten to the point that I just shut out their words and start praying for them, instead."

I was aghast that Sam and Sasha's fights were such a common occurrence that Mimi had developed a habitual response. "How often do they fight?"

She shrugged. "Last night was worse than usual. Have you looked around town, Gailynn? It's like Doc's dying lifted the lid off Pandora's Box. Everyone's at each other's throats. It's as if we're all afraid."

I shivered. Mimi knew the pulse of our community. Nothing happened in Hum Harbour she didn't hear about—usually before any of the rest of us.

"Afraid of what?"

"Just keep your doors locked, little cousin, and pray."

She washed her hands at the sink and dried them on a tea towel. "Instead of Sasha, maybe you could give something to Sam." She showed me a jar of mixed herbs. "I give this to the boys." I assumed she meant her dogs, not the men in her family. "It keeps them from wandering, if you know what I mean."

I laughed. "I don't think that's a problem. Sam loves Sasha. He's just being a jerk right now."

Mimi's brows shot up and I corrected myself. "OK, more of a jerk. I want something to help Sasha fight this depression she's in. You have something that will help, don't you?"

"My stock's a little low right now, but I'm sure I can find something."

Mimi checked five containers before she found two with enough stuff inside. She dragged out another mortar and pestle and began blending and crushing what she'd selected. Fragrance filled the room. She told me what the stuff was, but I honestly didn't pay much attention. Dead plants are all the same to me.

"I'm afraid there's not enough to make capsules but at least I can give you a tea. My new stock should be here any day. I'll let you know."

"Where do you order from?"

"All over. If it's from a Canadian grower, I order directly, but if I want something from outside Canada I get Sasha to order on my behalf. The flower shop imports a lot of plant stuffs, depending on the time of year. Sasha piggybacks my order to theirs. It cuts down on my cost."

She pulled out a small tin with a seascape stamped

on the outside, and dumped in the crushed leaves.

"I added mint to the mix since I know how fond Sasha is of mint tea. She can drink this as often as she likes."

"How much do I owe you?"

"For Sasha, nothing. It's the least I can do." Mimi snapped the lid on the tin and slipped it into a pretty blue-and-white gift bag. "Give this to Sasha with my compliments and like I said, when I have the other things I'll call you or drop it by Dunmaglass."

I departed, gift in hand. I'd wanted something stronger than tea, I mean, Sasha sure needed the help, but Mimi's tea was better than nothing. Hopefully it would take the edge off Sasha's misery. I smiled to myself, imagining what Doc would say. He'd been a firm believer in medicinal whisky for taking the edge off.

****

Sasha and Sam's house is a two-minute walk from Mimi's. I went there next, planning to brew Sasha a pot of Mimi's tea and help scour the house for her earrings. Even though I was sure she had nothing to do with Doc's death, I couldn't in good conscience lend her mine, but neither would I abandon her to Andrew when he was in his super-cop mode.

Sam's pickup was in the drive, unfortunately. Sam's company is never conducive to confidential sharing.

Banging once on the door, I let myself in. "It's just me."

My oldest brother lumbered into the front hallway from the living room, cradling an open beer in his hand. Our parents held very strong views about drinking and we'd been raised in an alcohol-free home. Sam's consumption of liquor was not the only parental dictate he'd spurned over the years.

"Sasha's still at the shop," he said. No hello, no how you doin' sis, just, Sasha's not here.

"The shop closed an hour ago," I corrected him.

"Then where is she?"

Her shoes were by the door. If he'd bothered to look he would have seen as much. "Aren't you worried about her, Sam? I am and so is Geoff."

"Well the two of you can mind your own business. Sasha and I'll sort things out ourselves."

"It doesn't seem to me like you are having a lot of success. Sam, she needs serious help before it's too late." I glanced towards the stairs. "Maybe she's up there."

He swallowed his beer.

"Have you checked?"

"What for?"

"Oh give me a break," I said and pushed him aside. Mounting the stairs two at a time, I called her name. No one answered.

I hadn't been upstairs in six months, but at that moment I didn't care how bad Sasha's housekeeping was. Ignoring the unmade beds, overflowing dirty laundry hamper and turned out dresser drawers, I checked each room, including the permanently closed door at the end of the hall.

To my unutterable surprise, when I opened it I discovered a magazine-perfect baby room. It was painted soft blue with a sponged rainbow curving from one wall across the ceiling to the other side, a Jenny Lind crib with this adorable little mobile, a change table stocked with unopened packages of disposable diapers, and a baby monitor on the painted dresser. Everything a brand new mom could possibly want in a nursery.

Sam hauled me back and slammed the door in my face. "You have no right to snoop in our house."

"Well somebody has to," I said and shoved him out of the way.

For one brief second before Sam arrived, I glimpsed Sasha huddled in the rocker in the corner with a plush pink teddy bear crushed to her chest. Tears glazed her cheeks, smeared mascara the only color on her face.

I pressed into the room and gathered Sasha into my arms. "Oh, baby," I murmured, holding her close. "What happened? Has Andrew been here already?"

Sasha silently uncurled her fisted fingers. One silver and violet seaglass earring rested on her palm.

"Andrew? What's he got to do with this?" my brother grunted.

"If you took any notice of things beyond yourself, you would know. Andrew's looking into Doc's death. He questioned Sasha this morning. He'll get to you, too, eventually."

Sam wouldn't enter the baby's room. "Sasha? What's Sasha got to do with Doc?"

"It's both of you, you idiot. It was you're bright idea to sue Doc, remember? Andrew is looking into everyone who might want Doc hurt, and your stupid lawsuit puts you and Sash at the top of the list."

Sam looked ready to run. Then he sucked in a deep breath and surged into the room.

"She's my wife. I'll look after her," he said, prying my hands from Sasha.

"It's too late for that, Sam. You go make us some of that tea I brought while I look after her. She's got to pull herself together before Andrew turns up."

At that precise moment, the front door banged open, followed by heavy footsteps downstairs.

"Hey, Sam, you here?" hollered Andrew.

"Stall him," I hissed. "Keep him downstairs till Sasha and I figure this out."

"Figure what out?"

Andrew shouted up the stairs. "Hey, Sam, is that you?"

I spun Sam around and pushed him out, shutting the door before he could react.

"Yeah, I'm here," I heard Sam answer. "You may as well come on up, too. We've got some party happening."

I turned back to Sasha. "That's it? You only found one earring?"

She nodded mutely.

"Does Andrew know?"

She shook her head.

I could hear Sam and Andrew arguing. So much for keeping Andrew downstairs until Sasha and I figured this out. Any moment he'd be barging through the door.

"It's no big deal if you've lost your earring, Sash. You have a legitimate reason for having been on Doc's boat. It doesn't implicate you in his death."

"Andrew won't believe that. Please, just let me use your earring. He'll never know the difference."

"I can't," I said. "It's wrong."

Ignoring me, she tugged off my earring.

I grabbed my empty earlobe in surprise. Sasha had actually ripped my earring right out of my ear. I reached for her hand but before I could nab it or say, "Give that back," Andrew opened the door.

"Ladies," he said.

I glanced at my sister-in-law, wondering if I looked as guilty as she did. I sure felt guilty.

"Did you find your earrings?" Andrew asked her.

Sasha held out a pair of seaglass earrings. I held my breath.

Unfortunately, Andrew knew us too well. His eyebrow rose ever so slightly and he looked me square in the eye.

"Gai?" Andrew read my reaction, and a very sad expression spread across his face.

He tucked my hair behind my ears "Where is your other earring, Gailynn?"

I couldn't speak.

"You had on two this morning. Is one of these yours?"

I hung my head.

"Why are you doing this? Don't you realize I could charge you with interfering in an investigation? Is that what you really want?"

I watched Sasha through my tears. What should I say? I wanted to ask her.

My friend slowly turned to Andrew. "It was my idea. Gailynn told me no, but I took her earring, anyway."

"Is that true, Gai?"

I nodded forlornly.

Andrew squared his drooping shoulders, as though preparing himself for an unbearable task. "Then I'm sorry, Sasha, truly, but I'm going to have to ask you to come with me."

"What?" Sam bellowed. "You're arresting my

wife?"

"No, Sam, I'm just taking her in for questioning. But if I were you, I'd call that high-priced lawyer you hired when you decided to sue Doc. Have him meet us at the station, just in case."

11

I was on autopilot, walking with my head down, paying attention to nothing except my thoughts.

Lord, why is this happening? Why is everything going wrong? Surely there must be something I can do to fix things, isn't there?

Lori pulled her dad's pickup to a stop beside me, almost running me over in the process. "Want a lift?" she asked.

I stared at her.

"I assume you're going home. Do you want a ride," she repeated.

I climbed in the passenger's side.

Lori looked me up and down before shifting the stick into gear. "What's with you? I haven't seen you look this miserable since you decided you were adopted. Remember that? You tried dying your hair red and somehow the peroxide turned it green? Then you had to tell your Mom why you'd done it."

I slumped lower in my seat. I was in grade six at the time and we'd started studying genetics. Mendel's square and all that. I was the only non red-haired MacDonald in three generations and according to Mendel, and my teacher, my two redheaded parents could not produce a black-haired child. That meant one of two possibilities: Dad wasn't my real Dad or both Mom and Dad weren't my real parents.

Dad had always called me his raven-haired maid, and I never understood how likening me to an oversized crow could be considered an endearment. When all this blew up Dad dragged out a box of old family photos and showed me the sepia-tinged picture of his grandmother. She was the daughter of a Mi'kmaq chief and her name, translated, meant Raven's Wing. I looked just like her, right down to the slant of my eyes. From that point on I abandoned my doubts, even taking modest pride in my poker-straight black hair and never questioned my parents again.

"Got plans for tonight?" Lori asked as she pulled into her driveway. "Would you like to stay for supper?"

Why not.

The Fisher's live in a basic three-bedroom bungalow, nothing fancy. Lori's mom kept it spic-and-span and Lori tries to follow in her mom's footsteps, but a housekeeper she is not. I added my shoes to the pile of discards stashed just inside the back door, hanging my jacket on top of several others already overloading the hooks.

I followed Lori into the kitchen and plunked myself into the closest chair. Like the rest of the house, the kitchen walls were covered with Lori's framed awards: piano, athletics, academic scholarships. Her dad displayed Lori's most prestigious trophies at the Bait 'n Tackle.

I propped my elbows on the table and rested my chin on my hands. A sweet smelling bowl of over-ripe apples and bananas sat in the center of the table. I stared at the tiny darting flies they'd attracted, pricked by some niggling thought at the back of my mind. I sighed. The connection would come.

Lori filled the kettle for tea.

"We're having leftover stew. That OK with you?"

"Whatever," I answered. I doubted I'd eat more than a bite or two.

Once the kettle and leftovers were on the stove, Lori drew out the chair beside me.

"OK, Gailynn, what gives?"

"Andrew just took Sasha in for questioning."

"Questioning? About what?"

"Doc. I guess Sasha delivered a gift basket for Doc before he set sail and somehow she must have lost an earring while she was on the Medical Convention."

Lori nodded. "That explains why Andrew wanted to see my pair."

"Did you show him?"

She pulled an apple from the bowl and began polishing it against her jeans. Her bandages rasped against the denim. "No, actually. Mine are somewhere in one of my boxes. I haven't bothered unpacking them. What with Geoff Grant buying Doc's practice out from under me, I'll have to move somewhere at the end of the summer. Much as I love helping Dad, I need a job that pays real money. Anyway, I offered to go through the boxes but Andrew said not to bother. As long as I had two earrings that was all that mattered."

"Yeah, that's what Sasha said, too. As long as Andrew could see two earrings that was all that mattered. Then she asked for one of mine."

"I don't see what the problem is. So what if she lost her earring on Doc's boat. Lots of people climb on and off his boat every day. Who cares?"

I frowned. Lori brushed aside Sasha's request as though totally irrelevant. I thought being asked to lie was a big deal. Did that make me naïve?

"I guess Andrew's trying to figure out who saw Doc last," I said.

"That's what he told me."

The kettle whistled and setting aside her apple, Lori made our tea.

"Andrew and Geoff think Doc's death is suspicious."

"Andrew told me that, too."

"What do you think?" I asked.

Lori clunked two mugs on the table. "I don't think what I think matters. Andrew's going to be looking for a motive and you have to admit Sasha has a good one."

"Her pregnancy?"

Lori nodded sadly. "Doc didn't have the skill to handle a high-risk pregnancy like Sasha's. She should never have left her OB in Halifax."

"But he told her it was safe to come home."

"Obviously he assumed she had access to a competent physician."

"Doc was competent."

Lori gave me that look, the one that means, 'you poor sucker'. "I know you've always been loyal to Doc, but honestly, Gailynn, by the end, his drinking was taking its toll. I wouldn't have been surprised if Doc had insisted on a hysterectomy, too. Now that would have cinched the whole disaster."

I chewed my cheek. Doc had scheduled Sasha for the procedure until Geoff unexpectedly turned up and cancelled the whole thing.

"That would've been bad," I had to agree. "Still, what's the chance of her ever having a baby now?"

Lori's dismissive shrug said it all. "I bet that's one of the reasons Geoff pushed Sasha and Sam to launch that malpractice suit."

"That wasn't Geoff's idea."

"Are you sure? I mean, who had the most to gain by the lawsuit?"

"I think Sam hopes for enough money to try the fertility clinic again."

"Well, yeah, but Geoff gets something out of it, too."

I looked at my friend in confusion.

"Haven't you wondered why he picked now to move home? I mean, sure it's fortunate for Sasha to have him back, but why now?"

I stared into my tea. I'd never told Lori how I'd opened my big mouth and, in a fit of remorse, confessed to Sash that Doc was drunk the night of her miscarriage.

"What are you getting at?"

"Well, consider this. Sasha calls her brother and tells him what happened to her. Geoff says wait a minute, Sasha, that doesn't sound right. I think you should consult a lawyer."

"So?"

"Don't you see? He pushed them into the lawsuit knowing full well Doc would be forced to retire."

"So?"

She pushed her chair back in exasperation. "Are you really that slow, Gai? He wanted to come home. He needed a job. He got one. I bet he wrote to Doc and offered to run interference if Doc sold him the practice."

"He was a missionary, Lori. You're accusing a missionary of blackmail."

She shrugged. "If the shoe fits."

Her words unsettled me. Lori had never been big into religion, as she put it, so I usually took her anti-

Christian quips with a grain of salt. But she had a point. It wouldn't be the first time a fellow believer chose a shortcut to serving God. I mean, did I honestly know what prompted Geoff to turn his back on what he'd once considered God's call in his life? I didn't know a lot about his years in Africa. Despite what he said at church, I doubted every day was filled with singing kids.

What if the fine lines around his eyes weren't from laughing or squinting in the sun? What if they indicated something darker? What if Africa had warped him? What if he was willing to do anything to get away from it?

"Go through Doc's old correspondence," Lori said, pulling me back to the present. "He should have kept a file of all that stuff. Check it out."

There it was again. Go through Doc's files. I'm not the kind of person who sees messages from God under every rock but this was twice someone had suggested I search Doc's records. Maybe I should take the hint. Except, of course, tonight was out because I couldn't get at the files, thanks to our carpet cleaner.

Lori took the pot off the stove and ladled healthy portions onto two plates. She brought them to the table while I grabbed cutlery.

"Isn't your dad having supper with us?"

"He's already eaten." She opened the cupboard door for me to see their blue recycling bin overflowing with empty whiskey bottles. "Honestly, Gailynn, I am at my wit's end."

"He drank all that?"

She nodded. "With the closure of the fish plant, business at the Bait 'n Tackle is way down. Doc and the guys convinced Dad a golf course was a sure moneymaker. It would solve all Dad's financial problems. So he went and invested Mom's life insurance money in that stupid golf course. Hum Harbour Holes, even its name is ludicrous. Who is going to take a golf course named Hum Harbour Holes seriously?"

"All of the money?"

She nodded again. "He actually thought he could make enough fast money to buy me Doc's medical practice." I knew from her tone she was quoting her father. "Instead he's lost his retirement fund and I'm refinishing that rotten old boat so we can give harbor tours. Tell me the truth here, Gai, who would pay to ride a lobster boat around Hum Harbour? Even if there was some magical golf course dragging in the masses?"

"The Holes are definitely cancelled?"

"Well who's going to pay for it? Doc's dead. No doubt his money will be tied up in probate for years. Dad's tapped out. And I heard Mike tell Ross you can't get water from a stone. So he's obviously not going to save the project."

"But I thought they'd all signed some kind of contract that guaranteed their investment if one of them died."

"I have student loans coming due. I'm in the hole big time, Gailynn, with no way out." Lori was evidently too focused on her own situation to hear my question.

"Everyone says there's a doctor shortage. Can't you get a job in Antigonish or New Glasgow?"

"You need money to buy into a practice, Gailynn."

"Maybe Geoff could hire you, part time, I mean. That would bring in some income."

Lori's eyes flashed. "Don't think for one minute I would even go crawling to Geoffrey Grant. That was supposed to be my practice and I won't give that thief the satisfaction of begging for crumbs."

I picked up my fork. Lori's determination to vilify Geoff was getting on my nerves. He was a nice man. He was Sasha's brother. He hadn't come home to Hum Harbour to sue Doc or ruin Lori's life. Those were simply unfortunate by-products of his return.

"I need to find another way to provide for Dad and me," Lori said.

And she would. Nothing kept Lori down for long.

Poking absently at the stew on my plate, I thought through our conversation. Despite Lori's comment that Sasha's behavior was no big deal, I felt concerned. Sasha was an honest, God-fearing woman who did not make a habit of tricking police officers. Grabbing my earring was out of character for Sasha. Lying to Andrew was unbelievable. She'd never behaved like that before. Was it guilt or the personality changes that went with her depression?

I swallowed the stew without tasting it.

I refused to believe Sasha had anything to do with Doc's demise. Which meant someone else did. Who? And why?

Taking Sam's malpractice suit out of the mix brought me back to Hum Harbour Holes as the most likely motive. Three men each lost a quarter of a million dollars, thanks to Doc. Which of the three might commit murder?

Bud Fisher, Lori's dad? Mike Johnson, Mimi's husband? Or Ross Murray?

I decided to start with Ross simply because I liked him least.

12

It's all very well and good to say I'd start with Ross Murray, but by ten o'clock the next morning I still hadn't figured out how. Nor had I gotten an answer the thousand times I phoned the S's.

You may not have noticed, but in Hum Harbour there's this odd pattern of couples hitching up alphabetically, at least the ones with lasting relationships. I don't know if it's somehow connected to the double H's in the town's name, but people around here actually buy into the silly superstition. Not me, of course, but others do.

Anyway, I kept calling Sam and Sasha, hoping to find out what happened after Andrew dragged them off to the police station.

Geoff and I rearranged the waiting room furniture after his clinic-opening prayer and although chicken pox still dominated business, the panicked rush seemed to be over. The day proceeded at a comfortable pace.

I used every quiet moment to sift through Doc's old files. It was a slow process. Ellen Fisher had been meticulous and over the years she had catalogued and filed every scrap of paper that passed over Doc's desk. Problem was, for some reason she hadn't differentiated between patient files and general business. I'd have to search every single folder in the cabinets!

By lunchtime, I'd checked through half of one drawer. At that rate, with four drawers per cabinet and eight cabinets in the room I'd be through Doc's files in twenty-four workdays or, roughly translated, one month. I needed a better system.

Geoff interrupted my search around the time I made that amazing deduction, and told me he was closing shop for the morning. Patients were gone.

"Scoot over to McKenna's and check on Sasha, will you please?" he asked. "I'm worried about her. And while you're there, why not order flowers for Doc's funeral? Whatever you think would be suitable from the clinic."

Apparently, one of his patients reported the service was set for Saturday.

****

McKenna's was crowded and everyone knew about Sasha's excitement. Trips to the cop shop for questioning did not go unnoticed in our town. And like me, everyone would come to the flower shop to see Sasha for themselves. Funeral flowers were simply the excuse we used to legitimize our visits.

Rickie Murray was first in line. She stood with her elbows resting against the glass showcase while she studied the imported crystal vases within.

Behind her, Vi Murray huffed impatiently. "They're funeral flowers, for pity's sake. Just pick something and let the rest of us have our turn."

Rickie is the third Mrs. Ross Murray, and anytime she and Vi, the second Mrs. Ross Murray, are within a hundred meters of each other sparks fly. Vi's dubbed their altercations The Murray Feud. According to Vi, feuding is a respected Scottish tradition, like caber tossing.

There's a considerable age gap between Ross and Rickie Murray. She recently turned twenty-five while Ross Murray is Doc's age. In fact, Ross's first wife was Doc's sister, Marjorie.

Marjorie divorced Ross when she caught him in a compromising position with his then secretary, Vi Hicks. Marjorie left Hum Harbour the day she signed the divorce papers. She's never been back, although perhaps she'd relent and attend Doc's funeral.

Vi was fifteen years younger than Marjorie and she stayed married to Ross a whole six months longer than her predecessor. She also produced one offspring, which Marjorie didn't manage either. Vi still lives in Hum Harbour. She spreads her alimony money around town like a gardener spreads manure, and everyone knows the way the wind blows when Vi's around. I think she enjoys raising a stink and embarrassing Ross as much as possible.

Rickie, the latest Mrs. Murray, was a casino cocktail waitress when she and Ross met. It was love at first sight. Ross fell in love with Rickie's exceptional twenty-two year old body and Rickie fell for his exceptional bank balance.

Rickie now cruises Hum Harbour in her sassy black MX-5 Miata, decked out in designer clothes, loud jewelry, and expensive dental work. She wears those invisible braces that I am told cost twice as much as the train-track variety.

That Ross's newest wife wears braces gives Vi endless fodder for making a stink. In fact, in the last three years there's not been a single public event that hasn't degenerated into a mud-slinging extravaganza.

This morning at the flower shop proved no exception.

Rickie pointed to the largest cut crystal vase. "What do you think, Sasha? One large arrangement or two smaller ones. You know, for each side of the casket."

Sasha looked at me helplessly. I could tell from the desperate ache in her eyes she was in no condition to decide anything for anyone.

Meanwhile, Vi peered over Rickie's shoulder. Her gaze zeroed in on the humungous rock on Rickie's finger like a Scud missile on a target

"When did you get that?" She said loud enough for all to hear.

Rickie casually extended her hand and studied the effect. "You mean this itty bitty little thing? Why, I really can't recall exactly when Ross bought it. He is sooo sweet. He's forever giving me pretty things." She drew out her vowels like a Mississippi Madame, which sounded absolutely ridiculous combined with her Cape Breton twang.

"Is that why he's refusing to send Ross Junior to camp this summer? Because he's buying you costume jewelry?"

Every summer RJ attended Campe Le Merr, an exclusive children's camp in Quebec.

Rickie spun around, bumping Vi back with her curvaceous—Vi claims enhanced—bosom.

Vi's eyes now latched onto the enormous gem resting in Rickie's cleavage. It matched Rickie's ring, and her earrings, which I spotted as her hair settled.

Vi grabbed the necklace and ripped it right off.

Rickie screamed as her hands flew to her throat. I could see the red streak where the gold chain etched her skin before it snapped.

"Give that back," she cried. "It's mine!"

"Not any more. Ross's obligations to our son supersede any arrangement he has with you. If he won't willingly fulfill his commitments to Ross Junior, I'll do it for him." Vi stuffed the gem into her purse. "Tell your husband I'm taking it to a pawn shop. If he wants it back he can get it there."

Rickie watched helplessly as the doors slammed behind Vi. "It is not costume jewelry," she declared, though of course Vi didn't respond. Glancing around the room, Rickie flipped back her hair to show off the ear baubles. "Ross insisted I have it for my birthday. But I swear I didn't know little Ross Junior was going to miss camp on account of me."

I couldn't help being curious. "What are you going to do?"

"Well, I don't rightly know. Normally I'd chase down that evil woman and take back what's mine. But if it's for Ross Junior..." Rickie ran her French manicured fingertip along the edge of the counter. "I always wanted to go to camp when I was a little girl but we never had enough money. I'd hate for Ross Junior to end up the way I did now that things are...*tight* for Ross Senior."

"Tight?" I asked in an equally conspiratorial tone.

"I really shouldn't say."

Rickie tapped the showcase glass, indicating a medium sized vase. "Two dozen white orchids please, in that vase, please." Then to me, "Unless you think one of your blown glass vases would look better?"

Rickie had never been inside Dunmaglass. I didn't realize she knew anything about my stock. "Why don't you stop by and see for yourself," I said.

"Before Saturday?" Rickie asked.

I admit it. I felt sorry for Rickie Murray. I couldn't imagine being married to anyone as old as Ross. She must be lonely for someone closer to her own age to talk to. I could be that someone. And besides, maybe Rickie was the answer to my dilemma, my way to find out about Ross. What had she meant when she said things were tight right now?

"Why don't you stop by tonight. You could shop and we could talk without anyone interrupting us. In fact, I'll put on some tea. Or do you prefer coffee?"

Rickie's eyes widened. "Why, tea would be just perfect." She purred the R. "Seven?"

"Seven would be lovely."

Finally, I was alone with Sasha. I rounded the counter and gathered her into my arms.

"Honey-child, you look like you could use a great big hug."

She ignored my horrible southern drawl and hugged back tightly.

"Gai, what am I going to do? I can't go on like this."

"You are going to hang on," I said. "You have people who love you and we are going to see you through this."

"I don't think I can."

I stepped back and gave her shoulders a little shake. "I won't hear any of that, understand?"

She bit her bottom lip.

"Last night, in the middle of all that mess I forgot to tell you I dropped off some of Mimi's tea. And she's promised she has more stuff coming that'll help you."

Sasha dropped her head on my shoulder and wept

"We'll get you through this, I promise." I hugged her again and, not the first time that day, or certainly not the last, I prayed God would work a miracle for her.

13

I finished sifting through that first file drawer by four-thirty when the clinic closed. No sign of Doc's Hum Harbour Holes contract. In fact, I'd found nothing remotely interesting, unless you considered stuff like Frank Ague's varicose veins intriguing.

On impulse, I jogged over to Sam and Sasha's. When I'd dropped by the flower shop Sasha was in no condition to talk and I was bursting to know the details of what happened at the police station the night before. I knew Andrew would puff out his chest and tell me his interview with Sasha was police business, stay out of it. Asking Sasha would only make her cry and she was doing enough of that without my help. So I figured Sam was my best shot for finding out.

I couldn't have been more wrong.

I could smell the booze before I opened the door. You'd think the house had been hosed down with it. My big brother ambled out of the living room, took one look at me standing in his front hall and, despite the beer in his right hand, strong-armed me right out the front door.

"You have no business sticking your nose into our lives." He bellowed loud enough for the whole town to hear. "Just leave us alone."

Sam waved his right hand wildly, smashing his bottle against the veranda rail. Beer, broken glass and

Sam's favorite cuss words spewed everywhere. Somehow in the process he even slashed his palm.

Furious, Sam chucked what was left of the bottle into the bushes bordering the veranda. "Come in my house again and so help me, Gailynn, next time it'll be your head and not my beer."

None of the MacDonald men are tall, but to a one, they're all built like stone walls: thick, solid and immovable. They can be tough, when they want to, and Sam especially, can be scary mean. It's not like my brother would ever do anything to hurt me, it's just when he's been drinking he projects this overpowering image which implies violence. At that moment, with blood running from the jagged cut on the palm of his hand, Sam looked downright frightening.

I thought perhaps it would be best if I left him to deal with his injury in peace. I even decided to forgo a parting comment, which is very unusual for me.

So, while Sam stood bleeding all over his front step, I turned tail and marched down the street. Quickly. Without looking back. And I didn't stop until I was home, safe, inside Dunmaglass, with Sheba crushed to my chest.

After about an hour, when Sam hadn't bashed down my door, and no one else called to inform me my oldest brother had just bled to death on his front stoop, I took my gathering bag off the hook and headed to the shore for my evening walk. Sheba came with me.

Tide was half in, half out, depending how you looked at it, and there was a fair strip of beach to scour. I took my time. The fleet was chugging into the harbor for the night, and the odd fisherman's voice rose above the drone of engines. Fishing was good so far this season. Most boats made their daily quota by late afternoon. The men unloaded their catch and were home for supper.

Lord, what's going on with Sam? If he'd only been out fishing like he was supposed to be, he would never have cut his hand, today. Is he all right, Lord? Should I have stayed to make sure?

Come to think of it, why *wasn't* Sam out fishing like he was supposed to be? I stooped and picked up a wedge of amber seaglass.

It seemed to me he was being extremely oversensitive about this whole police investigation business. As Lori said, there were any number of people who could have been on Doc's boat before he set sail. Sasha's earring was no guarantee she'd done anything untoward. So why get so upset? Tell Andrew the truth, answer a few questions and go home. Bring the lawyer if you really think its necessary, and be done with it. Let Andrew get on to the real suspects.

I scooped up a chunk of green seaglass and tucked it into my bag with the amber.

Maybe Sam's cut wasn't as bad as I thought. Maybe I overestimated the blood. I mean, I might not have been noticing things clearly either, seeing how unnerved I was. I'd never seen Sam that over-the-top mad before. Weird.

In fact, Sam'd been acting weird for months now, since Sasha's miscarriage, or maybe even before that. She'd needed him and he was nowhere to be found. I suppose he felt guilty. If he'd been there with her maybe he could have…

What, Lord?

Sam wouldn't have known what Doc needed to do anymore than I did. We required an informed medical person to tell us what Sasha and the baby needed and

Doc, our informed medical person of choice, had let us down.

No wonder Geoff came home to Hum Harbour. I bet once he heard what happened to his sister no plane was fast enough. Botched stuff like this might be par for the course in third world countries, but in Canada, we expect better.

Yes we do.

What if Sam's hand needed sutures?

I tugged my hair. A little pressure, a simple bandage, surely that was all he required. Besides, he'd be too stubborn to call Geoff and ask for stitches.

Sheba stalked a tidal pool on one of the granite rocks that slope along the shore. I stirred the shallow water with my finger.

Sam didn't want Geoff's help. Lori didn't trust Geoff, either. Did her concern about Geoff's motives bear considering? So what if Geoff approached Doc to sell his practice? What was wrong with that? Did it mean Geoff was up to something nefarious?

Well, God, did it?

I'd thoroughly searched Doc's A file and found nothing. Maybe his records for the sale of his practice would be filed under B for Bill of Sales. He'd never given me any contracts to file but if Ellen Fisher filed Doc's original purchase documents under B, maybe Doc slipped his new papers into the same folder. Of course the papers I sought could also be under P for purchase, M for medical practice, L for legal documents. Or they might not be there at all.

What if Doc kept his personal paperwork at home?

I had a zillion questions and no answers. What had Mimi said about Pandora's Box?

Crunching footsteps on gravel caught Sheba's

attention. Ears pricked, she turned her head to the sound. So did I. I did not, however, race to the source of that sound, namely Geoff Grant, or throw myself into his arms, as she did.

Geoff looked his usual handsome self with his coat collar turned up against the breeze and the blue-green scarf that matched his eyes. Lori called them shifty eyes, although I dismissed her criticism as a preference for hazel eyes, like Andrew's.

As I watched him approach, I wondered if Lori was right. What if Geoff was not what he appeared — the loving brother returning home to care for his only sister? Their parents both died while Geoff was in Africa and Sasha was all the family he had left.

Did that kind of aloneness drive a man to do uncharacteristic things? Did it change a man's character? Did I even know Geoff's true character?

I sighed. He'd been so nice to me, especially after the way I acted at church that first Sunday. It was as though he went out of his way to be charming. Lori would ask why.

Was it naïve to think he was simply a nice person?

He smiled at me now, the kind of smile that made my heart flutter, and I steeled myself against it. I was not naïve. Geoff Grant would not win me over with his easy smile and a few kind words. I was wiser than that.

"Gathering treasure?" he asked.

"Pondering life's mysteries."

He didn't respond, evidently waiting for me to elaborate.

"I have so many questions I don't even know where to start."

His smile deepened the clefts in his cheeks. "Why not start at the beginning?"

I hesitated. Was this another way to win me over? Listen to my worries and act concerned? Still, my main worries were my brother Sam, and Geoff's sister, Sasha. Between their marriage and Geoff's childhood friendship with Andrew, Geoff was practically family. What he didn't know about us would get lost in the small tidal pool beside me. Wouldn't his interest be logical?

"I stopped by Sam's to ask how things went at the police station last night. They hadn't answered the phone all day, and I was worried. Isn't that fair?"

Geoff nodded, though whether he agreed or just wanted me to keep me talking, I wasn't sure.

"Sometimes Sam makes me so mad, I could bash him over the head and not feel one iota of remorse."

Geoff tilted his head and his eyes darkened.

"OK, maybe not. But I swear that man is the most infuriating person God ever created."

"What did he do?"

"He threw me out of his house and told me to mind my own business." I didn't know why I shied from telling Geoff about Sam's bottle bashing spree. "He spent the whole day drinking, by the smell of him. Sasha is dying of misery, and he's so drunk he doesn't even see how much she's hurting."

Although he said nothing, I could tell Geoff agreed, so I rushed on.

"He does nothing. Nothing! Apart from suing Doc, which was the dumbest idea he's ever had, Sam's made a career out of doing nothing."

"He probably doesn't know what to do," Geoff said in his soothing doctor voice. "Depression can be overwhelming to live with."

"Exactly. Sasha is completely overwhelmed by it

so why doesn't he get off his duff and get her some help?"

"It doesn't work that way, Gailynn. Sasha has to want the help, herself."

"Well, how would he know if she wanted help, or not? I tell you, he doesn't care about anything besides himself. He ordered me to leave him alone. He was so mad he smashed his beer against the veranda. Broke the bottle!"

Geoff's eyes were suddenly cold as glacial ice. "He threatened you?"

I flapped a dismissive hand in the air. Two hours after the fact I was feeling cavalier. "That's just Sam sprouting off. He wouldn't actually do anything to hurt me."

"If there is any trouble, if you need anything at all, Gailynn, call me. I'll be over that rail to your place faster than an antelope over grass." He tilted my chin and held my gaze. The ice in his eyes was gone. "Understand?"

I blinked a couple of times. I wasn't sure at what point I'd jumped to my feet.

He dropped his hand and reached into his jacket pocket.

"I found these. Are they the kind of thing you gather?" He held a dozen pieces of seaglass in assorted shapes and colors. "I found most of them on the other side of the wharf."

"They're perfect. Thank you." He set the glass gently on my palm, and my hand tingled at the warmth of his touch.

"I see you out here every morning as the sun's coming up and then again at sunset. Do you like walking alone or would you appreciate company sometimes?"

I dragged my gaze out over the water. I wasn't having a lot of success with steeling myself, at the moment.

"I like the silence of the harbor, when there's only the gulls and me. It'll sound silly, but being alone out here makes me feel closer to creation, like I'm a part of the ocean, the wind, the earth." I shook my head. "I don't mean that in a 'Here I am Mother Earth' kind of way. It's just that when I'm alone I can feel God. Probably more so than any other time, even church. It's like—" I scrunched my nose trying to find the right words. "It's like when I touch the water or the wind, I'm touching God, and I can feel Him touching me. Is that weird?"

"It sounds holy."

"It does?" I felt myself blushing. Then I heard myself say, "If you're asking would I like company when I'm walking, the answer is yes; that would be nice, sometimes."

We strolled back to town and for most of the way I wanted to kick myself. How was I to objectively assess this man when I stupidly agreed to anything he suggested?

As though to prove my point, Geoff invited me to join him for dinner at the Hubris Heron and I promptly accepted. The restaurant would be toasty warm, a definite plus since my jeans were damp. The evening's special posted on the door said deep fried scallops, my favorite. And I could use the time to inquire into his motives. At least those were the reasons I gave myself for saying yes.

14

The restaurant is different in the evening. Mimi's at home with her kids, the lunch-timer crowd doing the same. Dinner at the Hubris Heron is turned over to high schoolers, rock music, lots of noise and testosterone.

We settled into the booth closest to the kitchen. Everything else was taken. The teenage waitress wore a white tank and black pants that clung so tightly they managed to cover everything and nothing at the same time. She grabbed the coffee pot and flounced to our table.

"Hi, Geoff," she said. She flipped over his cup and filled it without asking. "I thought maybe you weren't gonna make it tonight. Had to give away your table. Sorry." She looked me up and down.

"Hi, Stephanie," I said. I used to babysit Stephanie and her five malicious brothers when I was in high school. She'd grown up a lot. "How's school?"

"Fine." She gave Geoff her undivided attention while I got a view of her back. "Will you have the special?"

Geoff looked at me. "Gailynn, would you like to look at the menu?"

"The special's fine."

"Then make it two, thanks."

Stephanie heaved a sigh, "Whatever," and

reluctantly filled my cup, too.

Geoff and I watched her saunter away.

"I guess you come here often."

"Most nights I get Stephanie to pack up the special and I eat upstairs but sometimes I stay down here. The kids are noisy, I know, but after being away for so long I think of it as a crash course in Cultural Change."

"Have things changed that much?"

He glanced around the room and my gaze followed. The boys wore oversized hooded sweatshirts or white sleeveless undershirts and baggy jeans slung so low they defied the law of gravity. The girls squeezed into tiny tops and skin tights pants. Most, however, were not as pleasantly proportioned as Stephanie and although the overall effect might thrill the teen-aged boys present it did nothing for my appetite.

"What are kids like in Somalia?" I asked.

"Modest." He turned back to me. "Thanks for saying yes to dinner. I get tired of my own company."

"There's always down here if you're lonely," I said. I was sure Stephanie wouldn't mind, which annoyed me. The fact that it annoyed me, annoyed me even more. "Judging by the pictures you sent home to Sasha, you lived in a compound with hundreds of people. I'd have thought you'd be eager for privacy."

"You'd think. I shared a hut with six other doctors. We got along well enough, but you're right, there was no privacy."

"Kind of like Hum Harbour, where everyone knows everyone else's business?"

"It was a different kind of exposure. We knew each other intimately, if you're talking about sleeping patterns and irritations. But our thoughts, feelings, those are the kind of things you kept to yourself. A loose word overheard by the wrong person could have calamitous consequences."

Geoff fell silent as Stephanie arrived with biscuits and butter.

"What kind of consequences?"

He took a long time to answer. "Life is cheap in Somalia. For the meanest of reasons, anyone is expendable."

I shivered. Somehow, I knew that comment was significant. The things he'd seen had taken the luster off his ideal of helping humanity. I could see it in the deep lines in his face.

I'd hoped to uncover Geoff's motive for coming home. Maybe this disillusionment was as far as I had to go.

Once Stephanie set our dinner in front of us Geoff seemed to come to life again. "I've been thinking about Sam's reaction to you dropping by."

"I'm sure he's fine. We'd have heard if the cut was serious."

"What cut?"

"Didn't I mention it? Sam, uh, cut his hand when he was waving around the broken bottle."

Geoff laid down his fork. "Is there anything else you haven't mentioned?"

"Nothing significant. Sam's always been a bully. I'm used to it. Not that he'd ever be rough with Sasha," I added hastily. "He loves Sasha."

"Just because a man loves his wife doesn't mean he won't turn rough if he feels he's being pushed."

"He's never hurt Sasha, I'm positive."

He picked up his fork. "Neglect is another form of abuse. He and Sasha had been trying for that baby for years. The fertility clinic was their last option. Sam knew he should keep close to home until she was through the dangerous phase of her pregnancy. Where was he when she needed him?" His eyes glinted with anger.

Or was Sasha his reason for moving back?

"Did your sister ever tell you where Sam'd run off to?"

"No. But I get the sense that the men in this town take off whenever and wherever they like without much concern for their responsibilities."

"If you mean Doc, we always knew he was close. Most weekends he never sailed any further than Port Hawkesbury. He'd weigh anchor in some little cove and stay put 'til Sunday night, then sail home again."

"He's not the only one. Your cousin's husband, Mike, scoots off for days at a time."

"I've never heard Mimi complain."

"It's a pattern."

"I suppose." I thought of Ross Murray. If he'd stayed home and played ball with his son, I wouldn't be meeting the third Mrs. Murray after dinner.

"I learned to watch patterns of behavior in the camp. Sometimes that was the only warning you got."

"Warning of what?"

"Why do you really think Sam was angry with you this afternoon? It wasn't just Sam being a bully, Gailynn."

"Then what?"

"While I was away, Sasha wrote every week. She spent most of her letters talking about you, not her husband." When I didn't answer he continued, "Their marriage is in serious trouble."

I stared at my dinner. Serious trouble? I knew

Sasha was upset about not having babies, and Mimi'd told me Sam and Sasha argued from time to time, but I'd never considered it serious trouble. I should have, though. What kind of friend misses something that important?

"What's you're brother hiding?" Geoff asked.

I straightened. "Hiding? What makes you think my brother is hiding anything?"

"Like I said, I watch patterns."

I love my family, my community, and I pride myself in knowing everything that happens in my town—although it seemed I might be wrong about that. "What do you think Sam's hiding?" I asked, my ire rising.

"I don't know. But he had as much reason to want Doc dead as my sister might. More, if he's feeling guilty for deserting her."

"He did not desert her. He was just—missing in action."

"As long as he keeps drinking he'll stay missing in action."

Stephanie moseyed over and refilled Geoff's coffee cup. "Dessert?"

"Nothing, thank you," Geoff answered.

She departed without looking at me.

I stabbed my last scallop and scrubbed it into the tartar sauce. It was cold and tasted like day old newsprint. I wanted to spit it out, but I chewed and chewed and forced it down. I couldn't swallow the irritation seething inside me, though.

On top of everything else riling me, that sassy little sixteen-year-old was flirting with Geoff right under my nose. How dare she? And the only reason he ignored her was because he was too busy trying to frame my brother with Doc's murder…Well, maybe that was too strong, but he was throwing doubt on my brother's good name, implicating him in Doc's death. A few hours ago, I'd been ready to believe the same or worse of Sam, which only infuriated me more.

"Gailynn, are you all right?"

I glared at him. "Did you invite me to dinner so you could accuse my brother of who only knows what?"

He pulled back. Apparently that wasn't the answer he expected. "I invited you to dinner so we could get to know each other better."

"While a sixteen-year-old fawns over you?"

"What? Stephie? She's not fawning over me."

"Then what do you call it?"

He stared at me in obvious confusion, and I glared back, furious with myself for acting like a jealous fishwife. I couldn't believe I was acting like this. What right did I have to be jealous about anything in Geoff Grant's life?

He wanted to know me better well: here I was, Gailynn the idiot who constantly embarrassed herself by jumping to conclusions about everyone and everything.

My whole life my brothers have been telling me to mind my own business for this very reason. But I never listen. I just rush from one humiliation to another.

I hung my head. What must Geoff Grant think of me now? I wanted to discover what he was really like, deep inside. Instead, I'd proven beyond a shadow of doubt that I was the last person he should trust. Maybe that was also why Sasha never told me she and Sam were having marriage trouble. What had Geoff said about loose words and calamitous consequences?

"I'm sorry. Sometimes I overreact."

"You don't need to apologize, Gailynn."

"Yes I do. That was uncalled for."

"Yeah." A smile tugged the corner of his mouth and I found myself grinning back, my anger replaced by that now familiar stomach flip.

"What time did you say you were meeting Rickie Murray?"

18

Good question. What time was I meeting Rickie?

I checked my watch. When I first accepted Geoff's dinner invitation, I'd mentioned my seven o'clock appointment. Little did I imagine I'd be this reluctant to leave.

"Shall we do this again tomorrow?" Geoff asked.

"Walk and dinner you mean?"

He leaned back, his head resting against the booth's padded back, and smiled at me as though there was nothing on earth he'd rather do than sit there smiling at me. Which was ridiculous, especially after the way I'd just behaved.

"Walk and dinner."

Like every other suggestion he made, I agreed.

****

Rickie Murray's Miata was already parked in front of Dunmaglass when I left the Hubris Heron. She climbed out of the driver's side wearing spiky-healed leather boots, slinky jeans and a faux-fur trimmed, short celadon green leather jacket. Her pale blonde hair framed her face in perfectly sculpted layers, *tres chic*.

I wore thread-bare jeans, hiking boots and a water proof hooded jacket over the orange cable knit sweater Mom knitted me for Christmas three years ago, *tres ordinaire.*

She gushed a thousand thank-yous in her fake southern drawl as I ushered her into Dunmaglass.

Now I'll admit I'm partial, it is my shop after all, but whenever I step over the threshold and throw on the lights, I catch my breath. It was extremely gratifying to see my place had the same effect on Rickie.

The door closed behind us with its little bell chiming and Rickie sniffed the air. I perfume Dunmaglass with a subtle pot pourri, nothing brash like a candle shop, just a hint of spice. Dunmaglass is atmospheric, scarlet and amber glass, polished oak showcases and rough stone walls. I like to think stepping into Dunmaglass is like stepping into a mystery. Everyone knows about Brigadoon. Someday Dunmaglass will conjure equally mystical wonder.

At the moment the shop opened Saturdays and weeknights by appointments only. Come summer, I'd opened six days a week. Doc always employed summer hours at the clinic so I was able to open Dunmaglass from noon until nine every day—except Sunday, of course.

This year I anticipated an even busier summer than usual. Dunmaglass had been accepted into the Nova Scotia Tourism's booklet that features the best shops and studios in the province. I wasn't sure how I'd juggle the two jobs, but it would work out somehow.

Besides my seaglass jewelry, Dunmaglass features work by two internationally reputed glass artisans, Helena and Halbert Borgdenburger. They live up Murray's Mountain.

Helena creates stained glass. Three years ago, I

commissioned an original panel for Dunmaglass and when Helena saw her piece displayed in my large front window she asked if she could hang three other panels inside the shop. Helena's art resembles gothic windows. They fit my space perfectly and she sold all three that first summer. Next summer, same thing.

I now had three new ones hanging from the open rafters. With the light positioned behind each panel, they virtually glowed. Made me think of Rohan in Tolkien's middle earth.

Halbert, Helena's husband, creates blown glass masterpieces. Apparently glass blowing is a family tradition. I had four of Halbert's vases displayed on tall oak pedestals around the shop. They were also lit for glorious effect.

Compared to Helena and Halbert's art, I admit my jewelry is less grand. But I've arranged it on pierced black velvet and once again, light does the trick. Each piece of seaglass shines from within and the gold or sterling silver settings glisten magically, too.

Rickie wandered the shop, trailing her fingertip along the edge of each pedestal or showcase.

"Gailynn, these are sooo awesome I cannot begin to choose."

"Are you still thinking of one of Halbert's vases for your flowers?" Halbert's vases were works of art, sculptures worthy of a museum or art gallery.

"I had hoped," she said. "But now that I see them for myself... Do you think it would be in poor taste if I put the flowers in one of these vases and then asked for it back when the funeral is over?"

Yes. I didn't say that, though. Instead, "Doc has no family, except his sister Marjorie. She, being Ross's first wife, might make it a little awkward. What does Ross say?"

"Ross?" She put her hand to her heart. "My goodness, Gailynn, I would never ask Ross something like that. Why, the dear man would positively expire on the spot if he even saw the price on one of these itty bitty things."

"They are pricey," I admitted, "but Halbert Borgdenburger's work will only appreciate in value. They're an investment. Ross understands the importance of a good investment." What a perfect segue into my questions about Hum Harbour Holes. I could have kissed Rickie for making it so easy.

"Investment is rather a dirty word around our house, right now," she said.

Like I said, so easy. "Hum Harbour Holes, you mean?"

She waved that aside. "Every time I go shopping I tell Ross it's an investment. See these boots?" Graceful as a dancer, she swung her foot high and held it there while I appreciated the obvious elegance of her footwear. "Jimmy Choo. What could be a better investment than that?" She lowered her leg.

"Hum Harbour Holes?"

Rickie looked at me like my head was screwed on crooked. "The golf course? I don't think so. I heard Ross say—well, never mind what Ross said. It really wasn't important."

"Are you sure? Ross, Bud and Mike sank a lot of money into Hum Harbour Holes."

"Sank is right. Oh, don't tell anyone I said that. If Ross finds out I was talking about his investments he will be sooo annoyed with me."

My ears perked. "Is there a problem?"

"Besides Vi constantly picking on poor Ross and

demanding more money, you mean?"

"Sure, besides that."

She waved her perfectly manicured hands in the air. "Ross told me he cut her off because she's never satisfied. Never has been. No matter what he does it's not enough. And then today I hear about little RJ. Do you think she just said that to make me feel guilty?"

"You mean about Ross Junior not going to camp this summer?"

"Yes. Because I haven't told Ross she stole my necklace to pay for little RJ's camp. He would be so humiliated if anyone guessed."

"Guessed?"

"I heard about what's happened to Sasha."

I wasn't sure what that had to do with Ross's humiliating secret but I leaned closer.

"Everyone in town is talking and they are all saying poor Sasha couldn't possibly be responsible for what happened to Doc."

"No she couldn't," I agreed.

"She is sooo blessed. She has one itty bitty problem and everyone is there in a heartbeat to help her. Even her handsome brother flies all the way home from Africa and gives up on being a missionary so he can be here for her when she needs him. I wish I had the kind of friends and family Sasha has."

She asked to see a set of eighteen carat gold and amber seaglass earrings in the case. "I try, truly I do, but people in Hum Harbour have a hard time accepting anyone new." She held them up. "Vi doesn't help."

"I think most people turn a deaf ear when Vi starts ranting."

"You do?"

She looked so shy and hopeful I felt sorry for her.

"Are things really that tight for Ross?"

Rickie asked to see another necklace. "Can I tell you something, Gailynn? Will you promise to never tell another soul?"

I felt like a heel but I nodded.

"Things aren't going well for Ross. Selling Murray Enterprises was supposed to help, but it hasn't. And now that Doc backed out of Ross's silly little golf course agreement, well, Ross is nigh unto beside himself with upset."

'Nigh unto beside himself?' Where did she get this stuff? "Did you ever see their agreement, Rickie?"

"The papers? Sure. But I didn't understand what it was all about. I've only seen legal papers once before in my entire life, and that was when Ross asked me to marry him. Not that it will matter."

"Why not?"

"Because Ross doesn't have his fortune anymore."

16

By the time Rickie left she'd taken one vase on approval—I agreed to take it back if Ross hit the roof—two pair of earrings, a bracelet and an anklet, all with eighteen carat gold settings and chains, and my self-respect. I felt like an absolute creep. Somewhere along the way, Rickie interpreted my invitation to Dunmaglass as an overture of friendship. She was so desperate for a companion of her own age she'd misread my interest and told me things she had no right sharing. That I'd discovered Rickie to be a backwater kid like me who just wanted to be liked, only made me feel worse for wheedling those confidences out of her.

On top of that, Rickie didn't know any more about Ross's commitment to Hum Harbour Holes than I did.

So I gave her a deal on the jewelry and promised to make her another pair of earrings, whatever color she liked, as a gift. And I invited her upstairs for tea and a George Clooney movie, which we thoroughly enjoyed, and I also invited her to join Lori, Sasha and me next time we had a girls' night out.

By the end of the evening, I guess we really were building that friendship she coveted. As they say, sometimes God does move in mysterious ways.

****

Sheba and I were combing the beach by first light

the next morning. Salty mist fogged the air and I zipped my jacket up to my chin to keep out the damp. My eyes focused on the ground but my thoughts and prayers ping-ponged inside my head. My concerns weighed so heavy that no matter how hard I tried I couldn't seem to still my mind.

Lord, I know I've asked this so many times already, but please help Sam and Sasha. Bring them peace and healing. And don't forget Lori and her dad. They need you so much, too, Lord. How can I show Lori your love and forgiveness are real?

I scooped up a chunk of blue glass the exact shade of Geoff's eyes and held it up to the light. The thought of Geoff was enough to start my heart step-dancing against my ribs.

Then there's Geoff, Lord. What am I supposed to do with all these mixed up feelings he's causing?

I tramped on.

And Rickie, I know I invited her over last night to milk her about Ross, but You had something bigger in mind. Can I really be her friend and still suspect her husband of murder?

I was determined to find out who was responsible for Doc's death and Ross Murray, it seemed to me, was angling for position as my number one suspect. According to Rickie, the wealthiest man in Hum Harbour was wealthy no longer. Was that simply the way rich people talked or did Ross need Hum Harbour Holes to succeed as much as Bud Fisher?

Thoughts of Ross reminded me of Geoff's comment about how the men of Hum Harbour disappear every now and then. Geoff had a point. Where did these men go? What were they doing? Were their disappearances connected?

Although I told Geoff that Doc never sailed further than Port Hawkesbury, I didn't actually know that for a fact. True, he often weighed anchor in the coves near Hum Harbour, but there could be times he went further afield. How would I know?

And even if Doc was always aboard the Medical Convention drinking himself into oblivion, was Ross always off gambling? I knew he met Rickie at a casino, at least that's what Vi told everyone. Maybe Vi made it up so no one would like Rickie.

Consider also Mike Johnson. Just because Mimi never complained when Mike ran off, didn't mean Mike wasn't up to something nefarious.

Doc, Ross and Mike, three out of the four Hum Harbour Holes investors. What if they were all up to something nefarious together? What if they silenced Doc to prevent their secret from leaking out?

I froze in my steps. Was that possible?

Sheba and I reached the spot where Doc's boat ran aground. The Medical Convention was gone, with nothing left to mark the spot except a streamer of crime scene tape still tied to a tree. It lifted and snapped in the wind.

I saw movement among those trees and since I was directly below Ross Murray's property I called out, "Hello," in case it was Rickie.

Instead, Ross emerged from the trees. "Gailynn, you're out bright and early," he said.

As I've said before, Ross and Doc were contemporaries, but the two couldn't have been more different. While Doc had been tall and lean, Ross is short and stout. His shirt buttons strain over his belly, and I doubt if Rickie could reach her arms all the way around the man's middle. Doc's thick hair was steely gray and his eyebrows starkly black, while Ross's bushy blonde brows accentuated the artificial brunet of his comb-over. Doc's chin was dimpled; Ross's double. In essence, Doc was handsome and Ross is not.

"Rickie brought home a vase from your shop," he said. "Thinks we should put orchids in it for Doc's funeral. I said it was too showy but Rickie thinks a man's friends should be honored extravagantly."

"I told her she could return it if you thought it too expensive."

"She tell you it was too expensive?"

I toed the rock nervously. I'd learned a little of Ross's situation last night. Could I find out more? Dare I ask? "Perhaps I misunderstood what she meant."

He looked peeved. "Because if she did, she was wrong."

"Of course," I said in a tone that meant I didn't believe a word of it.

"You being sly with me, young lady?"

"No sir. I'm just concerned."

"What are you concerned about?"

"I'm concerned about what will happen to you and Rickie if Hum Harbour Holes doesn't pull though."

"What makes you think it won't?"

"Well, I know Doc backed out, which means your golf course is short of money."

"Who told you that?"

I hesitated. "I heard you talking at Doc's retirement party. Mike and Bud Fisher said they couldn't cover the loss when Doc pulled out and it sounded like you couldn't either."

His nostrils flared angrily. "So you invited Rickie to your shop to find out if I was broke?"

I felt my face redden. "She needs a friend and I thought I could be one."

He snorted derisively. "You're a lousy liar, Gailynn MacDonald. You should get your oldest brother to give you lessons."

"What's that supposed to mean?"

He shook his head. "I'm not going to answer your questions any more than I'm going to tell you how much money I have in the bank. But I'll warn you, young lady. If you're so all fire determined to stick your nose in other people's business, you better be prepared for the consequences."

I squared my shoulders so he wouldn't think he could intimidate me. "I'm not afraid of the truth."

"But you should be afraid of the people who are," he said, and then disappeared up the tree covered hill.

Be afraid of the people who are afraid of the truth. Who could that be? Less than forty-eight hours ago, I thought Hum Harbour was a supportive, happy community where no one harbored secrets. Boy, was I wrong.

17

Geoff didn't have any appointments that morning so he left me alone in the clinic while he visited his sister and ran a few errands.

I got back to checking Doc's files. I worked my way through B and C, looking for anything like a Bill of Sale for Doc's Hum Harbour Practice or a copy of the contract he signed for Hum Harbour Holes. Need I say my search proved fruitless? Why I ever thought I'd find something useful among his stacks of files I'll never know.

Frustrated, I stepped into Geoff's office, hoping I'd find what I wanted there. But in the few weeks Geoff had been at the clinic he'd already redecorated the office. The walls were a warm taupe, there were plants on the windowsill and framed photos on the wall. Boxes of Doc's old books were stacked in the corner, ready for shipping to Geoff's African mission. He'd told me medical books, even outdated ones, were precious to mobile clinics with no reference libraries.

In their place Doc's built-in shelves contained Geoff's books arranged in alphabetical order by subject. Some shelves, like immunology, were almost bare while others, like infectious diseases or oncology, were so crowded the books ran onto the shelf below.

I munched my bagel lunch while I perused them curiously. The diagnostic pictures in Infectious

Diseases of East Africa had me slamming the book back on the shelf and quickly looking for something less graphic. I chose Poisonous Plants of the Sub Sahara. It was soft covered with lovely color plates of plants in all their phases from seed to flower to leaf. I settled into Geoff's swivel chair and flipped through the volume, reading snippets here and there.

Maybe in the back of my mind was Geoff's theory Doc had been poisoned. I found Cinchona trees, which Geoff had mentioned. Apparently quinine came from Cinchona bark and a few years ago when it looked like Peru might run out of the trees, some bright entrepreneur decided to start Cinchona orchards all over the world. After all, malaria was on the rise and people needed quinine to treat malaria. I'd say the woman Geoff mentioned who died so painfully might have questioned the initiative, had she known.

Two plants on Geoff's windowsill were among ones listed in his book. I read through their write-ups very carefully. It would never do if some little kid decided to help himself to a leaf or flower. It was while I read about these two lovely little green plants that I remembered Lori's cautioning words.

Did Geoff have an ulterior motive for returning to Hum Harbour when he did?

It was like hearing Lori's voice in my head. Maybe Geoff decided it wasn't enough to remove Doc from Sasha's circle of medical care. Maybe he agreed with Sam; Doc should pay for destroying Sasha's last chance to have a baby. Geoff knew enough to make Doc's death appear natural. If Doc's boat hadn't washed up on our rocks no one would have been the wiser.

But the Medical Convention did wash back into Hum Harbour.

Next move: Geoff volunteers to help the coroner. And when Doc's internal bleeding comes to light, what better way to throw off suspicion? Suggest the weapon himself.

I threw the rest of my bagel in the garbage.

That's when Geoff walked in. He looked me in the face and then eyed the open book before me. "Find anything interesting?"

I closed the book firmly and stood. "Just looking for a little light lunch time reading."

Geoff took it from my hand. "If you're curious about poisons I have a couple of books that are more comprehensive. In fact, I've been going through them myself, trying to see what fits Doc's symptoms. If I can narrow it to a few likely possibilities, it might make Andrew's job easier. Who knows how long the provincial lab will take to analyze the samples we sent."

Either Geoff was such an accomplished liar he could run with any story without blinking an eye or he was what he seemed. Innocent. How could I discover which?

"Have you had any luck?" I asked. Maybe I could trick him into letting something slip.

"Too much luck, actually. Half the poisons listed cause internal bleeding. The trick will be discerning the ones most easily available here in Hum Harbour. I'm ruling out the more exotic poisons right off the bat."

"Now-a-days you can order anything over the Internet. I know Mimi orders some of her herbs that way. Why not exotic poisons?"

He shook his head. "Too time consuming. Whoever did this had the poison on hand. I think Doc's murder was a crime of opportunity, not something planned months in advance."

"There are poisons everywhere in Hum Harbour, car antifreeze, even those plants on your windowsill. According to the book I was reading, they're poisonous, too."

"Toxic would be more accurate. If you ate both entire plants down to the roots you'd suffer severe intestinal cramps but not much else."

"Did you smuggle them home in your suitcase?" I pretended to smile.

His eyebrows rose in surprise. "Sam and Sasha gave them to me as a clinic warming gift. She found them in a catalogue of tropical plants and thought I'd like them. I didn't have the heart to tell her they were toxic."

I baited him. "Didn't that make you wonder?"

"It's no big deal, Gailynn. Really. Those two plants are no more dangerous than Christmas Poinsettias or Easter lilies."

I tugged my ponytail. "Mimi told me she orders medicinal plants through McKenna's. Apparently, Sasha adds Mimi's order to their regular import orders. What if she ordered Doc's poison that way?"

"What are you trying to prove? That Sasha did murder Doc? I thought you were her friend."

"I am. That's why I'm worried. I know she's not herself, and so does Andrew." I dropped my voice. "We have to be ready to defend her against whatever he finds."

Geoff stuck the Sub Sahara Poisons book onto the shelf. I watched, wondering if he'd confess to poisoning Doc to save his sister. He didn't.

"I don't like where your thoughts are headed."

"If Sasha inadvertently helped the murderer by

bringing some exotic poison into the country, that person could just as easily leave Sasha holding the bag."

He spun on his heels, confronting me. "How many people are you prepared to falsely accuse?"

"I'm not accusing anyone."

"Sure you are. So far you've tried implicating me and your cousin Mimi."

I opened my mouth to deny his accusation then changed my mind. "Are you involved?"

Geoff's face twisted in disgust. "No! How could you think that? Are you so furious with me for buying Doc's practice? I know I ruined your dream of running the clinic with Lori, but do you hate me enough to think I'm capable of murder?"

I hung my head.

"I thought we were becoming friends. I thought you were starting to trust me."

"I was. I am." I threw up my hands. "I don't know." I felt like my words were poisonous, too. I was so ashamed I wanted to weep. "Why can't this just all go away? Why can't everything go back to the way it was?"

"Evil doesn't work like that. It doesn't slink off just because we want it to. It has to be confronted. Eradicated."

I blinked back tears. "That's what I'm trying to do."

"Then let me help."

"Because your sister needs you?"

"And because I need to, for me." He stuffed his fists into his pockets and studied his feet as though trying to decide what to say next.

"When I was in Somalia I turned my back on evil. I

was afraid so I ran home because I thought I'd be safe here. Maybe I am safe, but I can't live with being a coward. Let me fight this with you, Gailynn. Please."

I put my hand out to touch him, to reassure him, and found myself wrapping my arms around him instead.

That's how we were standing when Andrew and Lori walked in. Lori had on the smile she always wore when Andrew was near—the one I called adoring but my brother called beguiling—while Andrew looked, well, just plain startled.

Geoff and I jumped apart but not fast enough. I watched Lori's expression change from delight to undisguised shock, to stunning anger. I think she might have struck me had Andrew not grabbed her arm and hauled her back.

"Play nice, now," he said.

Lori clamped her arms tight against her sides. Her body was so rigid her glorious honey gold hair shivered with every furious tap of her toe.

I didn't know what to do. I was sure hugging Geoff must seem the ultimate betrayal to Lori, yet I couldn't explain my actions without betraying Geoff's confidence, in turn. And I wouldn't. I loved Lori very much, but I wasn't a fool. I knew how harsh her temper could be and at that moment, I chose to accept it rather than deflect it onto Geoff.

So all I said was, "It's not what you think."

"Then what was it?"

I couldn't think fast enough to lie so I admitted the truth. "I have no idea." This seemed to calm her and her toe stilled.

Andrew grinned. "I dunno, looks like a pretty clear case of sexual harassment in the work place to me."

I said, "It was nothing like that," and Geoff said, "Don't go there," at exactly the same time, which amused Andrew more.

"Do I need to be protecting my little sister's honor?"

"Don't go there," I said while Geoff, again at the same time, said, "It was nothing like that."

I decided to change the subject. "Why are you two here?"

"To see you," said Lori.

"To talk to Geoff," said Andrew. It was their turn to talk over each other.

Geoff held his hands up in a time-out T.

"Have you heard anything back from the provincial lab?" I asked Andrew. After all, Geoff and I had been discussing poisons before we were so rudely interrupted. Maybe Andrew had news.

"Sorry, can't discuss an ongoing investigation."

"That translates as no," Geoff said, "which means my books are still our best bet."

"Best bet for what?" asked Lori.

"We're trying to figure out what kind of poison Doc was given."

"Poison? I can't believe any one in Hum Harbour would poison Doc." She sounded disparaging.

I looked to Andrew. "Yeah, maybe you should be looking for a stranger instead of harassing the innocent people of Hum Harbour."

He glared at me and said to Geoff, "You're looking for our murder weapon among all those books? Good luck."

"Have you found any possibilities?" asked Lori.

"Gailynn wants to focus on the exotic, like

Ayahuasca from the Amazon. I'm thinking of something more local, like rat poison."

Andrew rolled his eyes at me. "How could anyone get Amazon poisons in Hum Harbour? You've got to be reasonable here, Gai."

"People import all sorts of things. Why not poison?"

"She has this bee in her bonnet," said Geoff. "Sasha does all the ordering for McKenna's, and Gailynn thinks someone could convince her to unwittingly order a poisonous plant and then be blamed for it. She's the perfect scapegoat."

Andrew pondered that. "You're saying someone at McKenna's wanted Doc dead?"

"She ordered stuff for everyone, even Mimi."

He shuddered. "You mean Sasha's responsible for that horrible tea Mimi keeps trying to feed me?"

"Are you saying Mimi's involved?" Lori asked me.

"Of course not. I'm simply pointing out how easy it would be for the murderer to do that."

Lori looked unimpressed with my logic. "Any medicine could hurt you if taken incorrectly Maybe Doc did it to himself, got careless mixing his meds with alcohol."

I chewed my cheek. "You're suggesting Doc accidentally poisoned himself? I think he was too experienced a drinker for that."

She spread her hands. "OK, then someone else. I'm not saying Mimi, but say someone who had access to her stock, what if they took something she would prescribe for its curative effects and gave it to Doc for another reason, never intending to kill him."

Geoff nodded. "Foxglove, for example. It would have a moderate effect a healthy person's heart, but for someone already taking digoxin it could be fatal."

"Does foxglove cause internal bleeding?" I asked. It was hard to imagine my favorite flower in my mother's gardens could be deadly.

Lori sniffed impatiently. "He was just giving you an example."

"Once the stuff's out of Mimi's hands is there any way to track it?" asked Andrew.

I pictured Mimi's bulging Rolodex. "She's very careful with her inventory. She keeps records of everything she has and who she gives what to."

"You'd have to go through Mimi's records and visit every person she's sold herbs to," said Geoff.

Andrew shook his head. "I don't see that as viable."

Lori's brows furrowed.

"What is it?" Andrew might not be head-over-heals for Lori, but he was sure attune to her moods. And when she spoke, he took it seriously.

Lori said, "You know, there's no guarantee Mimi's herbals are used the way she prescribes or for the length of time she mandates." She looked to Geoff. "How may times have you dealt with patients who quit taking their antibiotics after three or four days because 'they got better and didn't need them anymore'?"

"True."

"Who's to say the people Mimi gives her tea to don't just stick it in the back of a cupboard and forget about it? I'm saying tea but I'm thinking of medicinals like mandrake and turmeric. And I know Mimi gave Mom betel nut when she went through chemo. There's probably some left in our medicine cabinet. How many other people in town are like us?"

"Now you're suggesting I get a search warrant and confiscate every half used bottle of medication in Hum Harbour?"

"Only the stuff that causes internal bleeding," I said.

"Oh that's helpful, Gai. Real helpful." Andrew was sticking to his guns and keeping his part of the police investigation quiet. Although he humored us with talk of poison, he gave no indication which way he leaned officially.

He and Lori were right, too, when they said finding a potential poisoner in Hum Harbour would be impossible if we tried to trace an unidentified poison. Without the provincial lab's report, we were pretty well out of luck.

That took me back to motive and opportunity.

I came to a decision. Sort of. I decided to accept Geoff's innocence. I saw nothing to indicate he was even remotely involved in Doc's death, and I wanted to trust him, plain and simple. For Lori's sake, I would keep my eye on him, but I didn't anticipate finding anything to confirm her suspicions. Besides, keeping an eye on Geoff Grant sounded quite appealing, when I thought about it.

Sasha had both motive and opportunity, but I deleted her from consideration, too. And Sam, much as my brother infuriated me, I refused to think of him as a potential murderer. If I kept up like this, I would soon delete everyone in town.

Lori's dad had a motive, if you considered losing a quarter million dollars a motive. I knew nothing about means or opportunity for him, but I didn't think he could commit cold-blooded murder. Not Bud Fisher.

Mimi's knowledge and access to potential poisons

gave her means but she had no motive or opportunity. Scratch my cousin from the list. Her husband, Mike, however, had access to her means which, when combined with his motive, gave him two strikes. No denying, Mike was a possible suspect.

Then there was Ross Murray. I kept coming back to him. Though he hadn't admitted the loss of his Hum Harbour Holes investment would be disastrous for him, he'd been openly intimidating when we talked this morning. He'd warned me to be afraid of the people who are afraid of the truth. I inferred that to mean him. Did Ross have a secret worth killing for?

Lori, Andrew and Geoff were deep in animated conversation. Murder seemed little more than an intellectual challenge for them. For me, it was an emotional test; one I seemed to be failing. I hated that someone I knew might be involved. I couldn't eliminate everyone in Hum Harbour just because I loved them, which meant eventually I'd be hurt. It was simply a matter of time.

With great reluctance, I made another decision. I would check out Mike and Ross. Their involvement seemed the most problematic.

18

I excused myself from the think tank in Geoff's office and walked out without anyone noticing. I would start with Vi Murray. She was the perfect source because she knew everything there was to know about Ross.

Vi once worked as Ross's secretary at Murray Enterprises—the grand name Ross gave the family sawmill. Since their divorce, Vi had opened her own business. She did secretarial jobs around town, including working part time as Third Church's office administrator.

The church was around the corner from the clinic. I found Vi and Reverend Innes hunched over the church's ancient computer, trying to solve the latest problem with its Sunday bulletin program. My arrival seemed to herald a much-appreciated break. Welcoming me warmly, the reverend announced he was heading out for his afternoon donut. Did Vi or I want anything? We both declined and Reverend Innes scooted out the door, nabbing his coat off the coat rack on his way by. If I didn't know any better I'd think he'd been waiting for the first opportunity to escape.

Vi and I exchanged greetings and the appropriate amount of small talk, mostly about Geoff Grant, before I got to the purpose of my visit.

"You know how I hate gossip, Gailynn, but I think

in this instance you were right to come to me. You'd never know what was true and what was simply gossip if you asked someone else."

I nodded dutifully.

"Ross can be a very deceitful man, for all his charm." Her far away smile lit her eyes. Perhaps she was remembering the days when Ross focused that charm on her. "A man doesn't get far in business on charm alone, you know."

"So Ross is successful in business?"

"To a point." She leaned forward. "You're a sweet innocent, Gailynn. Growing up in Hum Harbour, you've lived a sheltered life. You've never been exposed to the baser carnalities of the human experience, and I envy you for that."

I wasn't sure whether or not I'd confronted baser carnalities since I had no idea what she was talking about. "What do you mean?"

Vi's round face flushed and she leaned closer still. "I don't want Reverend Innes accusing me of corrupting his flock, but you must watch TV, Gailynn."

"Of course."

"Then you know what kind of perversions a man is capable of."

My imagination flew in a dozen different directions at once. "Can't you be a little more specific, Vi? I don't want to entertain the wrong kind of perversion."

"Well, you've seen Rickie. Need I say more?"

I blinked. "Are you suggesting Ross is a pedophile?"

Vi straightened in horror. "Gracious, no! How could you think such a thing? I have a child by that man. You can't imagine I would knowingly co-habit with a—a pervert for heaven sake?"

"Not for a moment. That's why I'm asking, Vi."

She studied me, weighing the pros and cons of letting me guess 'til I got Ross's sin right. Apparently, she concluded, I needed guidance. Left to my own innocence, I'd imagine horrors too terrible for even her to contemplate.

"Ross is a compulsive gambler. All the Murray men are gamblers. I know they tell everyone Duncan Murray was chartered the land on Murray's Mountain by King George way back in 1793, but the truth is Duncan won the charter in a game of chance."

"What's that got to do with Ross?"

"Ross lost it in a game of chance."

"I thought he sold it to that German conglomerate."

"Well, technically he did. But the only reason he sold the mill and the mountain was because Ross's gambling had plunged him into excruciating debt."

"So Ross is broke."

"Worse than that."

"What could be worse?"

"You know that bauble Rickie gave me to cover little Ross Junior's summer camp?"

Saying Rickie volunteered the necklace seemed a stretch, but I nodded.

"It's a fake."

Her eyes shone when I gasped. "I know. It's terrible isn't it? They've only been together three years and Ross is already lying to her and taking her for a ride. He was faithful to me for over a decade before he started his shenanigans."

I settled back in my chair. "How important is it to Ross that his finances stay secret?"

"Are you asking if Ross would kill to keep them secret?"

"I'm hoping you'll tell me he wouldn't do anything of the kind."

"Then I think you'll have to leave the church disappointed, Gailynn."

"You think he would?"

"All I can tell you is about the day I overheard Ross and Doc Campbell arguing. Ross was still married to Marjorie, and I was merely his secretary, or so everyone thought. I can't say I'm proud of the way I behaved in those days, but God's forgiven me. I know it's all water under the bridge now."

"You overheard Ross and Doc."

"Ross's father, Jack, had just passed away and Doc came by with a copy of the death certificate. Ross needed proof of death in order to transfer some contracts into his name. At the time it seemed urgent."

"What did they argue about?"

"I'm not sure I should be telling you this, Gailynn. If Ross found out he could sue me for slander, or cut off his support payments for Ross Junior."

"I thought he wasn't paying them, anyway."

"Of course he is. It's just things like sailing camp and RJ's annual Christmas trip to Disney World that he's cut."

I held up my right hand, scout's honor. "I promise I won't tell anyone."

Vi pursed her lips. "What's the point of me telling you if you're going to keep this a secret?"

"I thought you wanted it kept secret?" I felt dizzy trying to keep up with her.

"Go through Doc's old files and look up Jack Murray's cause of death. If it's kosher then I haven't said anything slanderous."

"You haven't said anything, anyway."

"Well I've implied it. Ross is the father of my son and I won't be accused of falsely charging him with anything heinous."

I tugged my ponytail. "Vi, I'd hoped you could be more helpful."

"You thought I would lay Ross's secrets bare for the world to see?"

I felt lost. "You do that every time you see him or Rickie, in the grocery store, the bank, the florists."

"That's different, Gailynn." She shook her head. "If I can make Ross squirm after the way he cast me aside and humiliated me, I will. But divulging his secrets?"

I couldn't see the difference. "I guess I have a lot to learn about relationships."

"You do. In the mean time, be careful. Ross won't take kindly to you snooping. He's a very private man."

Great, I thought as I exited the church's side door. I already knew Ross was a private man, that's why I went to Vi in the first place. I figured she'd blow the lid off that privacy. I suppose she'd given me a hint, a lead I could follow. It wouldn't take long to check Jack Murray's file.

Andrew, Lori and Geoff were just leaving the clinic as I returned.

"Where have you been?" Lori asked.

"Running an errand." Vi's warning about slander kept my tongue in check.

"We've saved the world, and we're all heading in different directions. Andrew's got to get back to the Station but he's offered to drop me at the wharf."

"Want a ride?" Andrew, not Lori, made the

invitation.

"Thanks," I said, "but I still have a couple of things to do in the office." Lori rewarded me with a smile. I guess she'd forgiven me for hugging Geoff.

Geoff smiled down at me, too. "Whatever needs doing can wait until tomorrow."

I felt torn. Despite my aching curiosity, wondering what Vi'd been hinting, I could hardly insist on staying after my boss basically ordered me to call it a day. Besides, with the way his eyes sparkled, I didn't want to defy him. "I guess you're right," I said.

I did a chin point towards Andrew and the police cruiser. "Lori, better not keep the man waiting." It was the right suggestion because Lori hopped into the passenger seat without so much as a backwards glance. And I had Geoff Grant to myself.

"Are you going downhill?" I asked him.

"Indeed I am." We fell into step, Geoff shortening his strides so I wouldn't have to jog to keep up. "Your errand wasn't clinic business, I take it?"

"I needed to talk to Vi Murray. This morning Ross said something that bothered me and I wanted to find out what Vi might know about it."

"What did he say?"

"He told me I should be afraid of people who are afraid of the truth, which I took to mean him. I thought Vi might tell me what truth Ross was afraid of."

"I don't like you running off by yourself like that. You're ruffling feathers, Gailynn. One of these times someone is going to bite back."

"Mixed metaphors," I chided.

"Not if it's a peacock."

"Do they bite?"

He took my elbow, steering me away from the

middle of the street. "You're changing the subject."

"Is there a subject?"

"What did Vi tell you?"

I stuffed my hands deeper into my jacket pockets. "To check Jack Murray's death certificate. It may or may not indicate something suspicious, but that's actually what I wanted to stay back and do."

We reached Main Street and cut across traffic— two pickups and a minivan—and stopped to check out the latest rototillers in Hum Harbour Hardware's front window. Since neither of us needed a rototiller, we turned our attention to Mike Johnson and his brand new hybrid 4X4 truck idling beside the curb.

Vehicles are no more a priority for me than rototillers. While Geoff admired the engine's muted roar I took stock of the odd assortment of things Mike was piling into its flatbed: a duct-taped blue cooler, a pad-locked toolbox, a folded orange tarp, two shovels and a pickaxe. Curious, I thought as he headed inside the store for more.

"Do you want to go back to the clinic and check that file?" Geoff asked me.

Two minutes ago, I might have been inclined to say yes, but Mike's peculiar collection had my thoughts running in another direction. I mean, what did a cooler, toolbox, tarp, and digging implements have in common? The latest rerun of CSI flashed through my mind.

"Jack's file will still be there tomorrow," I said. "Do you have your car keys on you?"

He checked his pockets. "Yep. Got someplace in mind?"

"You did say you want to help me combat evil, right?"

He looked instantly suspicious. "Gailynn, what are you planning?"

"I'll wait here while you get your car," I said, unable to keep the excitement out of my voice. "I'll tell you then."

"Gailynn." He sounded stern.

"Hurry or we'll miss our chance."

I guess his curiosity won because he jogged away and two minutes later was back in his ten year old gray Corolla. And just in time, too, because as Geoff pulled in behind Mike's truck, Mike hurried out of the hardware store carrying a large camera case, jumped into his truck, and zoomed off.

I climbed in beside Geoff. "Follow that truck!"

Well, how could I resist?

19

Geoff stared at me slack jawed. "What?"

"Hurry or we'll lose him. I'll explain as you drive."

He threw the car into gear and the pursuit was on.

"Not too close. We don't want Mike to know we're following him."

"I hope you have a good reason for doing this."

I did. "You've been talking about the way the men disappear for days at a time."

Geoff pulled out onto the highway, careful to let two cars fill the gap between us and Mike. "So we're following Mike to find out where he goes?"

"Exactly," I said.

"What if he's just going for groceries?"

A rusted pickup pulled past us on the curve and I grabbed the dash. "Mike never gets groceries."

"Then where do you think he's headed?"

"I have no idea."

We drove for a bit, surprisingly content with each other's company. The scenery along that side of the cape always took my breath away and I stared out the window watching a small sailboat skimming the white tipped waves about a mile off shore.

We passed Cape George Lighthouse. "What else did Ross Murray tell you this morning?" Geoff asked.

"It wasn't so much tell, as accuse. He knew I'd invited Rickie over last night."

"I remember." Glancing sideways at me, he grinned. "You needn't worry. She's not my type."

I didn't care who Geoff Grant found attractive and I didn't want him to think I did. Even though I did. I stared out the window, piqued.

"You invited Rickie over," he prompted.

"She wanted to get a vase for the flowers she ordered for Doc's funeral."

"Aren't your vases a little pricey?"

"For some people, that's part of their appeal. Anyway, she was so glad to talk with someone her own age and she let slip a few things Ross didn't want spread abroad."

"Such as?"

"Apparently Ross is strapped for cash."

"Ross Murray? You must have misunderstood."

"That's what I thought, too. Then this morning Ross went up one side of me and down the other, accusing me of befriending Rickie under false pretenses. He said I was nice to her just so I could find out about his finances. Can you believe it?"

"I'm guessing from your display of righteous indignation he was right?"

I sighed. "Maybe. But in my own defense, by the time Rickie went home my friendship was sincere."

"I'm proud of you," he said. "I don't think your old friend Lori would reconsider any action she ever started."

True enough. Even when things backfired, Lori stubbornly stuck to her guns. There was that time back in high school when she bought one of Mimi's cookbooks after Andrew ranted about Mimi's desserts. She baked Mimi's famous walnut brownies, hoping to win Andrew's heart. Unfortunately for Lori, Andrew hates walnuts so he gave the brownies to Geoff. And when Geoff invited Lori to Spring Prom, Lori blamed Mimi for the mix up. She said Mimi knew the brownies were for Andrew, she should have warned Lori that Andrew hated walnuts. She caused such a fuss Mimi refunded Lori the cost of the cookbook plus five dollars for damages.

Maybe Lori's current dislike of Geoff stemmed back to that incident. She was worried he'd somehow come between her and Andrew again. Or maybe that he was coming between her and me?

Both possibilities unsettled me. I studied Geoff's profile and my stomach somersaulted.

"It was Ross's over-reaction that got me wondering if he was hiding something. I went to see Vi because I figured she would know."

Geoff slowed as another car passed us. "Sounds reasonable."

"But all she told me was to check his father's death certificate. Apparently Ross and Doc had a row about it."

"Nothing else?"

"That Ross sold Murray Enterprises to cover gambling debts."

"Interesting."

"And he buys Rickie fake jewelry."

Mike took the gravel turn-off at Georgeville, heading up the mountain. Geoff shifted gears. As his little car chugged up the grade, Mike disappeared around a turn. "I think this can officially be called a wild goose chase," he said, although he didn't sound particularly distressed. "We need a plan here, Gailynn."

"What do you suggest we do?"

"Have you got a camera? We could take pictures if Mike does anything suspicious."

Since I had none I said, "What else?"

"Perhaps we should have thought this through before we started."

"There wasn't time. It was move now or be too late."

Geoff drove silently. We followed the road up and down and around each twisting corner. Every now and then, we caught a glimpse of Mike's truck. Greening forest pressed in on both sides and we crossed a rapid flowing brook before we were looping back onto pavement.

"This is getting boring," I said.

"I don't know." He smiled at me. When I didn't smile back he continued in a cautionary tone. "It's better than dangerous. I've seen what cornered men are capable of and believe me, Gailynn, we don't want to push Mike until he feels forced to protect his secret."

"He's stopping!"

Geoff slammed on the brakes.

"Not here, around the next corner. If we pull over here, he'll see us. You can act like we have a flat."

I slid low in my seat as we zipped by him. Less than five minutes later Mike whizzed by us. Geoff tossed the car jack in the trunk and we resumed the chase.

"What did you see in Africa that makes you so concerned about cornered men?"

"War."

"That's it?"

"Isn't that enough?"

"I thought there might be more."

The road plummeted sharply and he gripped the

steering wheel until his knuckles turned white. "I'm not sure I'm ready to tell you."

"Is it that bad?"

"It takes time to establish that kind of trust, Gailynn. I'm not there yet." He braked. "But I'm working at it."

After a few more miles Mike pulled into Arisaig Provincial Park. The 'Closed for the Season' sign still barred the roadway so he parked beside the gate.

We stopped within sight of the Park entrance and watched Mike climb out of his truck. Camera case over his shoulder, shovel in hand, he disappeared up the path. Once Mike was out of sight, we coasted downhill and parked along the highway's shoulder.

"Let's go," I said, hopping out of the car. I was across the road and heading into the provincial park before Geoff caught up with me.

He grabbed my hand.

It was exciting, skulking through the pine woods, silent as the wind, which was actually noisy enough to cover our footsteps.

Mike carried something in his hand and he'd stop every now and then to consult it. Eventually he found what he was looking for.

Geoff dragged me deeper into the trees and we watched Mike plunge his shovel into the earth.

He dug a shallow hole and lifted out a metal box with reverent care. We couldn't see through his back and waited an eternity before he finally replaced the box in the ground.

By that point, I had to go to the bathroom so badly I thought I would explode. There were outhouses near the park entrance and I made a beeline for them as soon as I heard Mike start his truck engine.

Geoff checked which way Mike headed while I broke into the facilities.

"He's going back the way we came. Probably heading home," Geoff said when I came out. "Shall we follow or dig that box up for ourselves."

"Dig, of course."

Geoff used a fallen tree limb for a shovel and dug till he hit the box.

I held my breath, watching as Geoff mimicked Mike, lifting the box out, brushing it clean. What was inside? Drugs? Stolen jewelry? Pornographic photos? I mean, what did men hide in metal boxes in the woods?

Geoff flipped up the lid and we peered inside.

We exchanged confused glances.

There was a small, coiled note book and a Nova Scotia souvenir key chain. I'd seen a dozen such key chains beside the check out at Hum Harbour Hardware. Inside the note book were lists of dates, times and signatures. Mike Johnson was the last.

We sank back on our heels.

"That's not what I expected," said Geoff.

"Me either. What do you think it means?"

"I have no idea, but whatever this is, it doesn't look illegal. I think we're safe asking Mike up front." Geoff returned the note book to the box and reburied it.

****

The direct route home took about a quarter of the time. We drove straight to Mike's house and found his truck parked in the driveway. We pulled in behind him, effectively cutting off his escape. That was when we admitted the awkwardness of our plan. How did we uncover what Mike had been up to without confessing we'd spent the afternoon following him half way across the province— slight exaggeration.

I suppose you could say luck was on our side and we were saved the decision. Mike ambled around the side of the house, a coil of electric cable in hand, and grinned when he saw us.

"Was that fun?"

I tried to look innocent. "What do you mean?"

"Gailynn, you are one awful liar. But you're even worse at spying."

"Spying?"

He turned to Geoff. "She talk you into it? 'Cause I gotta say, if you're gonna make a habit of tailing people you need a better car. That old rattle trap is so noisy I could hear you behind me even when I couldn't see you."

"You knew we were there?"

"From the moment we turned out of town. At first I thought 'Hey what a coincindink, Gailynn and Geoff behind me.' But then you did that corny thing pretendin' you had a flat. You had my full attention then."

"Is that why you led us half way to Kalamazoo and back?"

"Yep." He looked pleased as punch.

"Was the digging part of your ploy, too?"

"Nah. That was the whole point of the adventure, least until you two made it even more fun."

"What was your original intention?" Geoff spoke for the first time.

Mike shook his head. "I dunno if I should tell you. I mean, then I might have to kill you 'cause you know too much."

20

The blood drained to my toes.

Mike grabbed my elbow. "Hang on there, girl. It was just a joke, a bad one, maybe, but just a joke."

Geoff pointedly removed Mike's hands from my person and led me to the front step. "Maybe you better explain," he said to Mike as I sank to my seat.

Mike scrubbed his hand across his chin. "Don't tell Mimi."

"Why not?"

"'Cause she's already got a head of steam up about how much I spent on my new GPS. And I told her I sent it back. If she finds out I kept the thing…"

"What's that got to do with today?"

He looked both ways. "I belong to this geocaching club. Call ourselves The Fellowship."

"What's that?"

"It's kinda like a car rally combined with a treasure hunt except there's no time limit," he said. "We connect through the Internet. Some geocaching groups are open to anyone but we're closed—with passwords, code names, that kinda thing—'cause of the size of our prizes."

"That key ring was a prize? It's not much."

"We're starting a new game. Last prize was a month long Mediterranean cruise. And the one before that was a quarter of a million bucks."

"How do you win?" Geoff asked.

"The fellowship leader buries a prize and posts the GPS coordinates on our website and we hunt for it. When we find the prize we sign in the book and exchange it with something slightly bigger."

"You left a five buck key chain."

"Yeah, and I got a two buck souvenir lapel pin."

"How does that turn into a Mediterranean cruise?"

"The cache I opened holds the coordinates for the next cache. It'll have a bigger prize. It goes up from there."

"There were a lot of signatures ahead of you," said Geoff.

"Yeah, I'm behind on this run."

"Mimi doesn't mind?"

"That I run all over the country? Nah. She hates how much I spend on the game, though." He frowned. "I'd about drained the kids' university fund when I won the big one. The quarter mill I mentioned? I invested that it in Hum Harbour Holes, thinking I could cover the loss and make enough on top to keep me going" He shrugged. "Guess not, huh."

I stared at him. "Why didn't you just put the money back into the kids' savings?"

"Lookin' back that woulda been a better idea but at the time I thought the golf course was a guaranteed investment."

"And now you've lost what you put into the golf course, too."

"I'm still optimistic. Ross'll come through with enough to cover Doc's part. You'll see."

From what I now knew about Ross Murray's finances that seemed unlikely.

"So you're not worried?" I asked.

"Concerned? Maybe. Worried? No way."

"What if someone told you Ross was broke?"

Mike looked me over. "Lookit, Gailynn, it's nothing personal, but I'd take what that someone says with a grain of salt. Know what I mean?"

I bristled. "No, I don't know what you mean."

He scratched his chin. "I know you like to think you know what everyone's up to, but this wouldn't be the first time you got things a little wrong. Remember that time you ran home screamin' Sam had murdered a vagrant? It turned out he'd been target practicing with your dad's BB gun and shot old lady McGuire's scarecrow."

I felt myself blush. "I was nine and I'd just learned the word vagrant," I explained to Geoff. To Mike, I said, "The thing crumpled and fell like a real dead person. What was I supposed to think?"

"Then there was the time you called the cops on Toby Pry."

"I saw someone break into his place."

"Yeah, but turned out Toby'd forgot his key and was sneakin' in the back window before his mama realized he'd snuck out."

"Your point is?"

"You've got some imagination, girl. If people took half your stories seriously we'd never leave our homes."

"I'm not that bad."

"There are people who think you are."

Mike had effectively changed the subject from Doc, Ross and Hum Harbour Holes, to me and my reputation for getting carried away. What if Geoff concluded I was a scatterbrained idiot and stopped helping me investigate Doc's death?

"I'm older now," I told Mike. "I don't fly off the handle over every little thing I see or hear."

He snorted. "Right. And that's why you had Geoff here wasting his afternoon following me when he coulda been doin' something constructive, like fixin' his apartment."

Geoff really hadn't seemed to mind. I glanced sideways, saw the way he shook his head ever so slightly.

At that, Mike threw back his head and hooted with laughter. "Bless my soul. Is that what a fella's gotta do to get a girl these days?"

I looked from Mike to Geoff. My confusion turned to surprise, then embarrassment, as I realized what the two were talking about.

I focused on Geoff. "Are you saying you don't actually care that someone in Hum Harbour murdered Doc? You're just pretending to be concerned? What do I look like, an idiot?" I asked, my anger spiraling.

If I admitted the truth to myself, I didn't for one minute think Geoff Grant could be sincerely interested in me as a woman. I wasn't smart enough or accomplished enough to attract a man like him, which, I suddenly realized, was exactly what I wanted to do.

"Now what will you do? Go laughing to Andrew? Or did Andrew put you up to this in the first place? Did he tell you to keep an eye on me so I didn't mess up his investigation?" I sprang to my feet, both humiliated and insulted. "If that's what this afternoon was about you can just forget it. I'm going home. You," I jabbed my finger at Geoff, "you can go somewhere else."

I stomped away.

****

I stopped at home long enough to grab my gathering bag and I fled to the shore. Sheba was nowhere in sight but I didn't worry. Probably waiting for tuna on Geoff's deck, traitorous cat. I stormed along the beach, ignoring whatever treasures might be underfoot. I ranted aloud all the way to the point, confident God could filter my words and pick out the salient points. Like, *When I asked You to deal with my feelings for Geoff You were supposed to take them away. Not make them worse! Is this Your idea of a joke?* And, *why am I always such an idiot? Lord, I go to church. I read my Bible. I pray. How come You're not making me a calm, logical human being? Isn't that the plan? You're supposed to be all-powerful. What's the problem here?*

The sun slid into the sea in a blaze of color but I didn't much care. I kept marching until I'd burned away my fury and shame. Unfortunately, there was no sign of any of the changes I was demanding. I guess I should've at least been thankful God didn't choose to answer me the way He answered Job.

Or maybe He did.

It was pitch-black dark by the time I got home. I let myself in the back door and climbed the stairs to my apartment.

No sign of Sheba, but I wasn't concerned. I filled the kettle and pulled a frozen dinner entree out of the freezer before I finally slid open my patio doors. I knew Geoff was home because the lights from his apartment shone onto his terrace.

"Hey Sheba, hungry?"

Something shuffled behind the giant flowerpot in the corner so I flipped on the deck light and called her again.

"Sheba?"

Being as I live across the street from a vacant fish plant I am aware that certain—shall we say uninvited?—vermin stroll through the neighborhood from time to time. My cat's a pretty good rat catcher but there is always the possibility she might miss a particularly intrusive rodent. The odd noise behind the planter suggested such a possibility so I proceeded with caution, tossing a cat toy into the corner.

The moan that followed chilled the fine hairs on the back of my neck.

"Sheba?" Huffing, puffing, I dragged the planter far enough out to get behind it.

Sheba crouched in the corner. She smelled like she'd rolled in fish guts. Her black fur was matted, her eyes glazed and dull. She tried to stand.

"Baby, what have you done?"

I dashed inside and grabbed a bath towel but when I tried to wrap her in it, she slithered bonelessly out of my grasp.

"Geoff!" My holler brought him running.

He vaulted the railing dividing our decks.

"What's wrong with her? Why isn't she moving?" My voice shook.

He ran his hand over her limp body. "Let's get her to the clinic. The vet's too far."

"Too far? What do you mean too far?"

He scooped her up and gently laid Sheba in my arms. "Meet me downstairs at the car. We'll drive."

"To the clinic? What's wrong with her? Geoff, tell me what's wrong."

"I'm not sure," he said over his shoulder. "I have my stethoscope and things at the clinic."

"Stethoscope? Is there something wrong with her heart?"

"Stop asking questions and let's go." He sprinted back into his apartment, slamming the sliding glass door.

My heart in my throat, I hurried downstairs. Geoff held the car door for me and once Sheba and I were inside he jumped in the driver's side. With a spit of gravel, he peeled out of the parking space behind the Hubris Heron. The clinic is two blocks away, a three minute walk or a thirty second drive. We were there in twenty. I followed Geoff into the examination room while he flicked on lights and grabbed a bunch of stuff.

"Put her on the exam table," was the only thing he said.

Geoff laid the stethoscope over her heart and listened. He placed it on her tummy and listened. He lifted her limbs and stretched them out. When he let go she just lay there limp as a dead jellyfish. He filled a syringe from a vial of clear liquid and gave Sheba a shot in the scruff of her neck. He went back to listening.

"What are you doing? What's wrong with her?"

"I'm not sure."

"But you gave her something. What did you give her?"

"Atropine."

"What's that for? Why isn't she moving?"

He held up his hand for me to hush. I held my breath.

"Better."

"What's better? Why do you keep doing that?" I meant shift the stethoscope here and there over her ribs and belly. He felt her ears. He wrapped the towel back around her, tucking in her limp arms and legs as though she were a baby.

"Let's go."

"What? Go? What are we doing?"

"Taking Sheba to the vet. She'll make it now."

I was in a daze. I had no idea what had just happened or why Geoff had done what he'd done but I clung to his words like a barnacle to a stone. She'd make it now.

We drove to the all night emergency vet clinic in Antigonish, sat there half the night waiting for the vet's verdict. She'd appear every now and then ask me a question and disappear again. Geoff held my hand through it all and when the vet finally announced Sheba was in stable condition and would probably make it, the dam holding back my tears ruptured.

Geoff hugged me close while I cried, and I heard the vet tell him he'd saved Sheba's life. Without the atropine to jumpstart Sheba's autonomic system, she'd never have made it to Antigonish.

"We'll keep Sheba until we're sure the poison's cleared her system and there are no residual effects but I think her prognosis is good," she said. "If she was a smaller cat I don't think we'd have been able to pull her through. Whatever they gave her was meant to be lethal."

I pulled myself free from Geoff's embrace. "You mean someone poisoned her?"

She nodded. "I'm afraid so."

I looked at Geoff in horror, realizing he'd already figured that out. Sheba had been poisoned. Like Doc.

Geoff drove us home around the time the sun was lightening the eastern edge of the sky, told me not to worry about work. There were only a couple of scheduled appointments; he could manage on his own. I didn't argue. I was drained. Now that I knew Sheba'd be all right it was like I'd nothing left inside to hold me upright. I practically crawled up my back stairs and collapsed on my bed. Dragging my comforter over me, I curled into a ball.

Someone poisoned Sheba.

Who would do such a thing? She was normally such a finicky cat, trusting no one except me and maybe Geoff. Who could get close enough to dose her? Who had access to her food? I was the only one who ever fed her, except for Geoff. If he hadn't been there to help, she would have died. But Geoff knew exactly what to do, fortunately.

If I hadn't been so upset and stayed so late on the beach I would have been home sooner. Maybe before she reached that near-death state and then I would have been able to get help in lots of time. The vet said the poison, whatever it was, would have killed a smaller cat.

I shivered. Maybe the poisoner hadn't miscalculated at all. Maybe he only wanted Sheba sick. Obviously, he knew Geoff was right next-door and would come to my aid. Geoff would know what to do.

In fact, Geoff even knew how to save Sheba when the poisoning went too far.

I stared at the ceiling while dawn crept into my room. I could hear voices down at the wharf as the men prepared to sail out for another day of fishing.

I thanked the Lord Geoff knew exactly what to do to save my Sheba.

My eyelids finally began to droop. Geoff knew what to do, Geoff knew what to do, ran through my mind like a hypnotic chant. I drifted asleep.

21

The phone roused me mid-day, the vet calling to say they wanted to keep Sheba another twenty-four hours to properly rehydrate her. I could pick my cat up Saturday. I felt edgy despite six hours sleep. I'd spent most of the time dreaming, or at least that's what it felt like, and my last thoughts had colored them, painting a collage of Geoff and Doc and Sheba, all wearing violet sea glass earrings. I didn't remember any more than that, but my knotted stomach assured me whatever else happened in my dreams it wasn't good.

Since I don't have a car I decided to scoot over to the wharf to ask Lori if she could drive me into town before Doc's funeral. At least that was my intention. However, when I went to let myself out of the house I noticed something unexpected. My back door was unlocked. Obviously, I'd forgotten to lock up behind me when I got home last night. I was somewhat distracted after all. I felt my coat pockets for my keys and, wouldn't you know it, they weren't there. After some frantic searching I located them upstairs on the key hook beside my fridge.

This, unfortunately, meant I hadn't locked the door when Geoff took Sheba and I to the vet either. Dunmaglass had been open all night.

I raced downstairs so fast I missed the bottom two steps. Grabbing the stair rail was all that kept me from spilling onto my nose. And a good thing, too, because when I saw the shattered glass strewn across the shop's floor I almost collapsed.

The showcases' glass had been smashed and my jewelry tossed in every direction. Worse, however, were Halbert Borgdenburger's beautiful, one of a kind vases. Shattered. Shards of scarlet and amber glass everywhere.

I ran to the bathroom and vomited. Then I called the police.

Andrew came with sirens blazing.

The lunch crowd from the Hubris Heron stuck their heads out to see all the excitement.

Andrew shooshed them away.

Lori abandoned scraping the Lori-Girl and hurried over; he let her stay.

"Convenient," is what Andrew said as he stood in the middle of Dunmaglass surveying the damage. "Coincidental, too, don't you think?"

I sat on the stairs, my head between my knees. I wanted to wail. "What am I going to do?"

"Insurance will cover your losses, Gailynn." Despite her impatient tone, Lori's arm around my shoulders warmed me.

"But what will Halbert say when he sees what's happened to his vases? He'll never let me show any of his work again. And Helena will take her panels home and I'll have nothing but my jewelry."

"They're only a couple of vases, Gai," said my brother.

"Only? Do you have any idea how much they cost?"

"A lot?"

"Twelve hundred each!" I wrapped my arms

around my head and moaned. "Who could do such a thing?"

Andrew had his flip pad in hand and was scribbling madly. "Who do you think?"

"A monster. A philistine. A vicious hoodlum who has no appreciation of art."

"Anyone in particular come to mind? Anyone who might want to hurt you?" Andrew asked.

"Sam, Ross, Mike, take your pick." The names popped out of my mouth before I had a chance to censor them.

Andrew latched onto the list. "What makes you think they would do anything like this?"

I explained about last night and Sheba and how Geoff had saved her from certain death.

Lori's brows formed a deep V. "I don't suppose Geoff had any reason to poison your cat himself. There'd be nothing to gain, except maybe your undying trust when he just happened to be around to save her."

Both Andrew and Lori ignored my indignant gasp.

"Not worth the trouble," said Andrew. "But poisoning the cat so someone could break into Gailynn's shop might."

"You think the two are connected?" I asked.

"Too convenient for them not to."

"But why?"

"Let's talk about the three you mentioned. What have you been up to that would make you think Sam, Ross, or Mike would do this?"

"Sam's mad at me because he thinks I'm meddling."

Lori looked me up and down. "Are you?"

"Whose side are you on?"

"Both of yours. I want to find out who did this as much as you do. You're my friend, Gailynn, and I don't like you getting hurt."

Andrew nodded. "For now, at least, whoever is doing this is just using scare tactics. They're giving you warning, Gailynn. Stay out."

"Stay out of what?"

"What are you meddling in most?"

I did not meddle.

"I told you to keep your nose out of the police investigation into Doc's death. Are you?"

I didn't answer.

"OK, what did you do yesterday when Lori, Geoff and I were talking?"

"I went to see Vi," I said reluctantly.

"About?"

I shook my head. "It's too complicated to explain."

"Try me."

Lori's bandages scratched when she squeezed my hand. Sanding her dad's boat was wreaking havoc on her knuckles and palms. At this rate, by summer's end she'd be applying for skin grafts.

"Go ahead. Tell him," she said.

I stared at my feet for a full minute trying to word my statement in the least incriminating way possible. I wasn't having much luck.

"Rickie came by and bought one of Halberd's vases for flowers for Doc's funeral and she happened to mention that she and Ross are having a cash flow problem. I guess Ross is really the one having the problem although it affects Rickie, too, because she likes to invest his cash—"

"Gai."

"Well, then Ross got mad at me because I'd invited

Rickie for tea when I was just trying to be nice because she's very lonely." I added, "She's actually a nice kid, Lori, and I thought we could invite her along next time you, Sash and I have a girl's night out—"

"Gailynn." Andrew said my full name louder, as if I'd not heard him last time.

"Ross got mad at me because he thought I'd invited Rickie over to milk her for information about him and, isn't that just like Ross to think everything's all about him? I admit I felt bad, and in a way he was half right because I did find out about them being strapped, but he told me that wasn't true and that got me to wondering which one of them was telling me the truth."

Deep breath.

"So I went to Vi because Vi knows everything about Ross and she told me yes Ross is in a financial pickle because he's lost all his money gambling and he had to sell Murray Enterprises and he needs Hum Harbour Holes to make money so he can go back to buying Rickie real diamonds instead of fake ones."

"Rickie's rocks are fake?" asked Lori.

"Apparently the one Vi stole off Rickie the other day at the florists is fake because Vi didn't get anything for it when she tried to pawn it to pay for Ross Junior's summer camp."

"Hold it. Vi stole Rickie Murray's diamonds?"

Lori and I nodded.

Andrew reviewed his note pad. "So let me capsulize this. Sam is mad at you for meddling in his marriage and Ross Murray is mad at you for meddling in his marriage."

"I don't meddle."

"How about Mike?"

"I don't think Mike's mad at me."

"You said Mike."

"Yes but when I think about it, Mike didn't seem upset at all that Geoff and I spent the afternoon following him. I think he thought it was rather funny and as long as we don't tell Mimi what he was up to, I don't think he cares one way or the other."

"You spent the afternoon following Mike?"

"Geoff has this idea that the men around town just come and go as they please without concern for kith or kin and it struck me he's got a point. So I thought if we followed Mike and saw what he was up to maybe there might be a connection to Doc. You know, like a secret worth killing for."

Andrew slammed his little book shut. "Gailynn, you have got to be kidding."

"No."

He massaged his brow as though he had a splitting headache. "You can't keep doing this. Tell her, Lori."

"Gailynn, you can't keep doing this."

I pushed her arm off my shoulder. "You always side with Andrew."

"I do not."

Andrew interrupted us. "Let's get back to the break in. Geoff was with you at the vets so we can eliminate him as a suspect. I'll check alibis for Sam, Ross and Mike."

"It could have been kids," said Lori, though I could tell from her rigid shoulders that she was miffed about me being with Geoff.

"Maybe you should dust for prints," I said to Andrew.

"How many people have been in and out of

Dunmaglass since the last time you wiped down your cabinets?"

"I dust every morning before I open the shop."

"I mean wipe down with soapy water."

I sheepishly admitted at least a week.

"Then I really don't see much point in checking prints. Half Hum Harbour will have spread their finger marks through this space."

Lori said, "How about the vases? Hardly anyone handles them."

Andrew surveyed the carnage on the floor. "This isn't CSI you know. I collect all the little bits, send them to the provincial lab and next year some time when it's quiet someone might get around to examining these pieces of glass."

I almost started crying all over again. "You have to send them to Halifax?"

"You think I have a lab set up in the coat closet at the station?"

"I just sweep it all up and that's it?"

"I'll take photos and fill in a report. You forward a copy to your insurance company but yeah, Gai, that's it."

"Except for Andrew's lecture," said Lori.

****

Andrew and Lori left me cleaning up the mess. I wept as I swept. How could anyone do this to me?

Although I'd told Andrew I thought Sam, Ross or Mike were responsible for the break-in, I had a hard time believing it. I simply could not get my head around the evidence before me. Someone was out to get me, Gailynn Elizabeth MacDonald. Why?

Was I getting so close to someone's secret that I made them nervous? I surveyed the room. This was more than nervous. Nervous people had eating disorders. They spread gossip. They made anonymous phone calls or slipped nasty letters under your door. They didn't break into your shop, poison your cat and trash thousands of dollars worth of stuff.

Was I getting close enough to the truth to warrant this kind of a warning? No more "Mind your own business, Gailynn." No more "Go away or else." No, whoever was responsible had decided to move beyond words. He was acting.

Which begged the question: whose secret was I closing in on?

Sam? Was there some deeper issue between Sam and Sasha that my brother did not want me messing with? Did Sam have a secret even Sasha didn't know about, and Sam was afraid I'd uncover it and tell? Would my own brother poison my cat?

Or Ross? Ross needed money. To me that might be nothing more than a curious bit of news, but for Ross, was it a secret worth fighting for? Did his financial difficulties have bigger implications than I could understand? Were compulsive gambling and womanizing his only vices?

Then there was Mike. What if that GPS treasure hunt thingy was a smoke screen? What if he was involved in drug smuggling or something else equally illegal? How far would Mike go to protect Mimi and the kids? And speaking of Mimi, how far would she go to protect her family?

Mimi had access to Geoff's apartment. She could easily slip upstairs and stick something questionable in Sheba's tuna. And she was in and out of the Hubris

Heron's back door so many times a day who would notice her checking out my back door? Who would question her if she slipped out of the restaurant for five or ten minutes to trash Dunmaglass? I stared at the pile of shattered glass. Would it even require five minutes to make this kind of mess?

But Mimi? Was my cousin capable of this kind of destruction? Absolutely not, I told myself. Then I remembered Mimi remorselessly pulverizing poor bits of dried leaves with her mortar and pestle. OK, Mimi could smash stuff.

Was she the culprit?

Had I solved the mystery?

I weighed the possibility, unsure if I should be worried or excited. I felt both at the same time and that frightened me. I should be frightened. Any intelligent person would be frightened. Why then, did I feel excited, too? A sure sign I lacked the brains God gave me, Andrew would say.

I let the idea sit for a while, like a spicy candy melting on my tongue.

Using my needle-nosed pliers, I cautiously extracted my jewelry from the pile of broken glass. Halbert's vases had fractured into dangerously long slivers, and I didn't want glass splinters under my skin. I was glad there were only three vases in the shop at the time of the break-in. At least I could give him Rickie's twelve hundred.

I called my insurance broker who promised to stop in before supper and assess the damages, and the glass people said they could replace the plate glass in my showcases early next week. They had the measurements on file.

I prayed before calling Halbert Borgdenburger and

that prayer, at least, was answered. Hal took the news better than I ever could have expected. He even suggested I have the paper send over a reporter and photographer to cover the story.

"Big news," he said. "You never know who will read about the break-in and think, 'I've never been inside Dunmaglass. Maybe I should make a special trip to Hum Harbour.'"

"You think a break-in will attract customers?"

"Absolutely. I'll bring by four new vases and some smaller pieces, if you're interested, of course. When do you expect to reopen?"

I blinked in amazement. "Next Saturday. I won't have new glass in my showcases before then."

"That will be fine."

The Casket, Antigonish's weekly rag, asked me not to clean up anything before their reporter photographed the shop. I said yes of course, and went to work scattering the broken pieces back across the floor.

The mail arrived while I was mid-sweep. It included Rickie's check with insufficient funds stamped across her childish signature. I guess that proved once and for all that the Murrays were indeed in financial trouble. Could it be Ross who trashed my shop?

I phoned Rickie, explained the bank problem. She laughed and promised to drop off a new check. I'd never had to confront someone for non-payment before. I think I was more humiliated than Rickie.

After that, I sat on the dryer in my storage room, awaiting the reporter. What should I do now? Keep snooping, knowing I was getting under someone's skin, and pretend I wasn't scared? Heed the vandal's warning and leave Doc's murder for Andrew the cop to solve? Invest in one of those noisy security systems and hide inside my home for the rest of my life?

Well, God?

This was too big a decision to make on my own. Who could I go to for advice? Scratch that, who could I go to for advice I'd listen to? That was always the problem, wasn't it? Who would I listen to? Who could I trust to advise me honestly without the pre-assumption that I wasn't smart enough to do what needed doing? That I wasn't smart enough to recognize I wasn't smart enough, should have been a clue, don't you think?

22

Lori was not on the Lori-Girl. With Mom and Dad out of town I'd thought she was my best choice for wise advisor and gone looking for her as soon as the reporter/photographer—one person with two hats—left. The fishing fleet was still out. The wharf was deserted, apart from the gulls.

Seeing that Sam's boat was gone along with everyone else's, I decided now was an ideal time to visit Sasha. She'd be closing the flower shop and I'd have her undivided attention.

I hurried uphill and caught up with her as she walked home. She looked terrible.

"Are you drinking that tea I brought you? Mimi said it would help."

"And Geoff's pills. He said they'd take a few weeks to kick in. Should I have told him about the tea?"

I shrugged. "Maybe it'll make the pills work faster. When do you expect Sam home?"

"Not before dark, he told me."

That was interesting. Sam usually came and went without telling Sasha anything. Maybe recent events had snapped him out of his careless attitude towards his wife. "Shall I keep you company?"

I cooked Sasha a nutritious supper then, over her favorite dessert of ice cream and maple syrup, I quizzed her about Sam.

"Do you ever wonder where he goes when he takes off without telling you?"

Sasha's kitchen window overlooked the harbor. She ignored the view and dug in her ice cream.

"I mean, he told you today what time he'd be home, but that's something new isn't it?"

She took a slow bite and nodded.

"So how come the big change? Did Andrew's arresting you scare Sam into taking better care of you?"

"Andrew didn't arrest me. He brought me in for questioning."

"But is Sam afraid Andrew might change his mind and arrest you? Is that why he's sticking close?"

"There's no reason to arrest me, Gailynn."

"I know that, but does Sam?"

"Yes, he knows."

She said it with such certainty I felt my eyes go wide. "Sash, are you saying my brother is guilty?"

She looked sincerely surprised. "Sam had nothing to do with Doc's death. Why would you think that?"

"Sam was so angry with Doc and he was going to get away without paying the malpractice suit. Who would be surprised if Sam got drunk enough and angry enough to do something stupid?"

"I told you, Gai, Sam wasn't involved."

"Are you sure? He drinks so much. He's acting like he's guilty about something."

She pushed her ice cream away. "I know. But it's my fault, not his."

"Your fault?"

"It's complicated, Gai. You don't want to know all this stuff."

Oh yes I did. "Maybe it'll make you feel better to

talk about it."

"It's been going on a long time. Sam and I haven't been happy."

I knew that much. No one could watch two people they love go through the kind of heartache Sam and Sasha had been through during their ten years of marriage and not see their unhappiness.

"The first few childless years were tough, but we both thought we'd get through them. We were young, healthy. Surely we could produce kids eventually, right?"

I nodded.

"After a while I got really scared, though. I mean, what if we couldn't do it? What if *I* couldn't do it?"

I reached for her hand.

"I tried everything I could think of, from taking my temperature ten times a day to sleeping with my feet in the air...don't laugh." Sasha seemed unable to meet my gaze. "I finally convinced Sam that we should try that fertility clinic in Halifax. And it worked. The doctor at the clinic warned us I might not be able to carry the baby to full term but we were riding so high. I mean, finally, at long last, I was pregnant. I knew if we just followed his list of do's and don'ts, we would end up with a fine, healthy baby. When we came home we took their list of instructions to Doc so he could double check everything they told us."

"What did Doc tell you?"

"He said their instructions were unnecessarily cautious. I was in good health. Now that I was finally pregnant there was no need for concern beyond any normal pregnancy."

"But you were still cautious."

"Of course. I wasn't going to take any chances. But

Doc told Sam I was overreacting."

I ground my teeth. I loved Doc, but there were times…

"I was so scared we'd lose the baby after all we'd been through, and we'd never be able to try again if it didn't work. It cost so much. So I stewed, I fretted. I pushed Sam away. I was so worried something might go wrong that I didn't want him near me."

I stared at our intertwined fingers, unsure whether I wanted to know this much about my brother's marriage.

"Sam couldn't handle it. He started seeing someone."

I definitely didn't want to know this much.

"I don't know who, but at least she wasn't from Hum Harbour. I couldn't have borne it if she was someone I knew, someone I saw every day."

I swallowed the bad taste building at the back of my throat.

"That's where he was when I had the miscarriage. That's how come no one could get hold of him."

If my brother had been in the kitchen I would have belted him in the nose, I was so angry about the way he'd treated his wife, my friend. He'd betrayed her. He'd betrayed all of us. Unable to sit quietly and take any more revelations I started collecting dishes.

"He feels so guilty," Sasha continued. "He thinks it's his fault everything happened. If he'd paid more attention to me, if he'd been home when the cramps started, he thinks he could have made sure Doc saved the baby."

I wanted to scream: he's right!

"If I hadn't pushed Sam away he wouldn't have been with that other woman in the first place. Don't you see?"

"Is that why you've been so miserable? You think losing the baby is somehow your own fault?"

"Isn't it?"

"No! Lori told me pregnancies like yours are notoriously unstable. No matter how careful you are, they often just don't work. Doc telling you to ignore the clinic's instructions wasn't helpful, but there was nothing he, you or Sam could have done to prevent your tragedy."

A tear traced down her cheek. "Sam said it was my fault." She dropped her head into her hands.

"Well it wasn't, and my brother is an idiot. I don't know why you put up with him." I left the dishes in a pile and pulled a chair close. My arms around her shoulders, I laid my head against hers and we cried.

It didn't prove Sam hadn't busted up Dunmaglass, but now that I knew Sam's secret I realized it didn't give him a motive to hurt me. The one Sam wanted to hurt most was Sam, and he was doing a knockdown super job at it. Drinking, lazing around the house, avoiding work, those were all self-destructive behaviors. Thanks to Andrew and this whole Doc situation, however, it appeared maybe Sam was finally coming out of his funk and taking his life back.

Please Lord, don't let it be too late for Sam and Sasha.

23

It was going on ten by the time Sam and the fleet got back from fishing, and I went home.

Sheba was at the clinic until tomorrow. Dunmaglass was dark and empty. I flicked on every light, threw open every cupboard and closet door, to prove to myself no one was lurking upstairs or down.

The sudden blaze of light attracted Geoff, who leapt the rail and banged on my patio door. Once I pried my heart out of my throat, I slid open the door and invited him inside.

"Where have you been? Andrew told me what happened to the shop. Why didn't you call me?"

Geoff's over six feet, which makes him significantly taller than the other men in my life i.e. my brothers and my dad. The way he loomed over me, seething with pent up I-don't-know-what, sent me scurrying to the safety of my kitchen.

"Would you like some tea?" I asked, filling the kettle.

"No. I want answers."

I turned to plug the kettle into the stove and bumped into Geoff's chest. Cold water sloshed out of the kettle's spout, soaking the front of his shirt. He gasped and jumped back.

I kept the kettle between us. "Why are you so worked up? It wasn't your place that got trashed."

He sputtered. "Why am I worked up? Someone broke into your home. You could have been hurt. You could have been attacked in your sleep. You could have been killed."

"Andrew figures whoever ransacked my shop did it while we were at the vet's."

"But he doesn't know that for sure. Gailynn, don't you grasp the seriousness of this?"

I waved the kettle threateningly. "Don't treat me like an imbecile."

"Then don't act like one."

The words hung between us...sizzled would be a more apt description, actually.

I set down the kettle very slowly. "You can leave the same way you came in."

"Gailynn, I'm sorry. I didn't mean to call you an imbecile."

"Well you did. Go."

"I was frustrated. I was worried. I couldn't find you, and no one knew where you were. Not Andrew. Not Lori."

"You called my brother?" Until then I hadn't thought I could get any madder.

"What was I supposed to think? You'd been gone for hours. You weren't answering your phone. Your place was dark."

"So you called my brother?"

"And Lori."

As if that made it better? "You had no right treating me like a child and calling Andrew."

"I was scared! I thought something had happened to you!"

"Well, nothing has. I'm fine. I had a nice supper with your sister and then I walked home. End of story.

So now you can turn around and go home the way you came."

"I don't want to go home. I want—" He blew out a breath. "I need you to believe I did not mean what I said."

"Then why did you say it?"

"Because I'm an imbecile."

I felt the corners of my mouth twitch. "Yes, you are."

"Will you forgive me?"

"Will you promise to never call my brother on me again?"

He did a three-finger salute and tried to look penitent.

The tension eased.

I felt more kindly disposed towards the worried doctor. "Would you like some tea? I could tell you what Sasha told me about my debaucherous brother."

"Debauched, you mean. Yes, thanks."

"You knew already?"

"Knew what?"

"That my brother's been stepping out on your sister. Sasha says it's over and Sam's promised to never do it again, but I don't think she's sure whether to believe him, or not. Can a woman trust a man when he says something like that?"

"I think it depends on the man. Do you trust Sam?"

I hated to admit my uncertainty. "Normally I'd say maybe yes, but after what's been going on in their lives...It'd take a very callous man not to be moved, wouldn't it?"

"Tell me what's been going on," said Geoff.

So I did.

He sank into the couch and propped his socked feet on the coffee table beside mine. Geoff sighed when I'd told him all.

"You think that lets Sam and Sasha off the hook for Doc's murder?" he asked.

"I want to. Shouldn't I?"

"I don't want to think them guilty any more than you do, but where does that leave us if we eliminate them from consideration?" He put his empty mug next to his feet.

"With Hum Harbour Holes. Ross, Mike or Bud killed Doc because he pulled out of the investment."

Geoff wagged his head from side to side, as though weighing the idea's validity. "Money's always been a time honored motive for murder."

"I vote for Ross," I said.

"What have you got against Ross Murray?"

"He's a compulsive gambler and a skirt chaser. And any man who'd marry a woman young enough to be his daughter is a letch as far as I'm concerned."

"Don't hold back, Gailynn. Be honest about how you feel."

I wrinkled my nose. "Can you tell me he's an honorable, trustworthy man?"

"I don't know the man well enough to make that kind of judgment."

"Well, would you marry someone half your age?"

"That would be illegal."

"You are being intentionally obtuse."

He smiled at me. "Would I marry Rickie Murray, is that what you're asking?"

I wasn't sure I wanted to hear his answer. "Sure. Would you?"

"Not in a million years."

"Why not? Rickie's…" I let my hands drop in embarrassment. "I thought that's what men look for in a wife."

"When I look around Hum Harbour it strikes me Ross Murray is the only one who looks for that in a wife."

"What are you looking for?"

He slid his arm along the back of the couch, angled himself to see me better. "Are you pumping me, Gailynn MacDonald?"

"I honestly want to know. If not beauty alone, how about beauty and brains, like Lori."

"Now I know you're pumping me. Remember that one time I took Lori to the prom? Believe me, one date with Lori Fisher was enough to last a lifetime."

"Are you celibate then?"

His eyebrow quirked. "Yes I am. Are you?"

This wasn't supposed to be about me. "Not that it's any of your concern, but yes, I'm saving myself for marriage even though it'll probably be someone like Dale McKenna. Don't laugh."

He wasn't. "Dale McKenna?"

I plucked self-consciously at the lint on my jeans. "Well, I just think we're doomed to marry each other since no one else will ever want us."

"Don't sell yourself short."

"Now you sound like my mother."

"You sure know how to cut a guy," he said, hand to his heart.

I felt confused. "I didn't mean it as an insult. I just meant it was a nurturing kind of thing my mother would say."

"You're making it worse."

I picked up my mug, slurping down the last cold

dregs of my tea. "Can we please change the subject?"

"Not yet. Do you really think Dale McKenna is the only man who would find you attractive? Don't you see yourself when you look in the mirror?"

"Who do you think's our most likely suspect?"

He tilted my chin with his fingertip. "Because when I look at you I see a very attractive woman."

"Maybe we should consider an alternate theory of the crime."

"Don't you believe me?"

"What if Doc had some secret skeleton in his closet and someone decided to kill him out of revenge? Or, better still, what if someone was afraid Doc would expose their skeleton?"

"Will you believe this?"

He took my face between his hands and he kissed me. Just like that.

I didn't know what to say. I didn't know what to feel. My heart pounded, my fingertips tingled, of all things, and what I really wanted to do most at that very moment was lick my lips and savor the taste.

He slowly let me go. "Gailynn."

I took our empty mugs to my little galley kitchen before I embarrassed myself. The clock on the stove said three minutes to midnight.

He sighed heavily and followed me. "I think you should stop worrying about who killed Doc and start worrying about your own safety."

"I'm well aware this is serious business. I don't know why you and my brother seem so convinced I'm unable to grasp something that simple."

"I didn't mean to imply that."

"Of course not. But you do imply that every time you brush aside my thoughts."

"A kiss is not brushing you aside."

Then what was it? I watched my knuckles turn white as I gripped the edge of the stove. "It's been a long day. Maybe it's time we called it a night."

"Gailynn, we need to talk about this."

I felt close to tears. "Not now."

"Are you crying? Have I made you cry? I didn't mean—"

"Go home, Geoff."

I felt his uncertainty, felt him watching me, heard him walk away. It wasn't until the sliding door clicked shut that I turned away from the stove.

****

What was wrong with me? I'd just been kissed by the handsomest man in Hum Harbour and I couldn't stop crying. Was I having some kind of breakdown?

I sat in my dark apartment, hugging my knees to my chest, sniffling and shivering. I was scaring myself. I'd been like this for over an hour. Maybe it had nothing to do with Geoff's kiss at all. Maybe it was delayed reaction to Sheba's poisoning and the break-in downstairs. Maybe I was a useless write-off, like my brothers thought. Maybe I was losing my mind.

I blew my nose, adding the wet tissue to the growing mountain beside me, and reached for the phone. I needed comfort. I needed assurance. I called Lori.

I woke her up, of course.

"Do you know what time it is?"

I blew my nose.

Her bed sheets rustled as though she sat up. "What's wrong? What's happened?"

"I can't stop crying."

"I can hear that, Gai. Have you been robbed again?

Have you called the police?"

"Geoff kissed me."

Silence.

"I don't know what to do."

"Well, usually when a man kisses you, you kiss him back if you liked it, or you slap his face if you didn't," she said tersely.

I blew my nose again.

"OK, Gailynn, what did you do?"

"I told him to go home."

"Did he?"

I nodded, then said, "Yes," since she obviously couldn't see me.

"Then what's the problem? Or is that the problem?"

"I don't know what the problem is, that's why I called you. I thought you could tell me what's wrong."

"Gailynn, have you been drinking?"

I gasped. "Of course not. Why would you think that?"

"Because you're not making any sense."

"I know. That's what's scaring me." I sucked in a hic-coughy breath. "Lori, I want to knock down his door and beg him to kiss me again and that's so awful."

"It is a bit cheap, I'll give you that. But I'm not sure it's awful, unless, of course, you actually do it."

"But he stole Doc's practice from you. How can I want to kiss someone like that?"

"True. You're being incredibly disloyal to find him attractive. I thought you were a better friend than that."

She was teasing me, trying to lighten my mood. It didn't help.

"I'm so sorry."

"Gai, it was a simple little kiss, right? Not a marriage proposal? Then don't sweat it. Chalk it up as another Gailynn MacDonald conquest and go to bed."

Easy for her to say, she made conquests wherever she went. Me, I'd never had one my whole life, unless you counted the time Dale McKenna caught me behind the funeral parlor when I was eight.

"Gailynn, you've had a rough twenty-four hours. You're exhausted, that's why you're not making any sense. Make yourself a cup of warm milk, drink every last drop and then tuck yourself into bed. You'll be asleep in no time and everything will look better in the morning. Trust me. I'm a doctor, remember?"

"Lori?"

"Yes?"

"What does it feel like to be in love?"

For a minute, I thought she was going to hang up on me.

"Have you got anything stronger than warm milk in your house? Because now, you're starting to scare me, Gailynn."

"No. Is that how it feels? Frightening?"

"Are you afraid of Geoff? Is that what's bothering you? You like him but you're afraid he might be behind Doc's murder?"

"Of course not. Should I be?"

"You know him better than I do, Gai. What do you think?"

I didn't know what I thought. That was my whole problem. I did what she advised, though, made myself some warm milk and crawled into bed and eventually I did fall asleep. But as for things looking better in the morning...?

24

Not quite.

Saturday morning, the day of Doc's funeral, was miserably wet. Nova Scotia weather is like that: beautiful weather all week then everything goes to pot on the weekends. As I walked the beach, I spotted Geoff watching me from his deck. He didn't join me, which I guess was wise on his part, but disappointing nonetheless.

Beneath him, the Hubris Heron's back door stood wide-open allowing Mimi's succulent aromas to drift seaward. Saturday mornings were big business at the Heron. Mimi cooked an incredible brunch and people even came from Truro to partake. My cousin would be occupied 'til mid-afternoon when she planned to close the restaurant and attend Doc's funeral.

A few doors further along Main Street stood Hum Harbour Hardware. I could see the back lot with its stacks of lumber, and the forklift loading prefabricated trusses onto a flatbed truck. Mike was the only one allowed to operate the forklift. He'd be busy all morning, too, no doubt.

I trudged homeward, damp and treasureless. Although Lori'd promised to run me into town before noon to pick up Sheba I still had hours to wait. It was barely eight o'clock and I had nothing but fretful thoughts to fill my time. So when Mimi popped her head out the Heron's back door and flagged me over, I went willingly.

"Gailynn, you're the exact person I've been hoping for," she said. "I wasn't sure what I was going to do."

While Mimi worked her way through the conversational preliminaries, the scent of sizzling bacon and fresh perked coffee had my mouth watering.

"Edna Sinclair's going to be calling and I forgot her geranium cream at the house. It's in the jar on my worktable and I am so swamped there's no way I can run home and get it. Mike's at the hardware store, the kids are sleeping over at, well, to make a long story short, would you be a dear and scoot up to the house and fetch it for me?"

"It's all ready to go?"

She nodded. "Just grab one of those gift bags out of the cupboard, you know where I keep them, pop the cream into the bag with one of my cards and bring it down here to the restaurant. I'll give it to Edna at the funeral."

"Wouldn't it be easier if I just dropped it by her house?"

"Would you?" Mimi flung her arms around me. "You are such a love. Whatever would I do without you?"

Edna Sinclair, Third Church's organist and choir director, is a sprightly eighty-one-year-old who prides herself in her youthful complexion. She credits it to twelve hours of uninterrupted sleep every night and Mimi's geranium-infused face creams, of which she'd apparently run out. Definitely a serious predicament.

"Just set the bag inside her back door," Mimi said. "Edna'll know what it is and she'll be so thrilled I haven't forgotten her."

As I've mentioned before, Hum Harbour is a lock-free community. Apart from maybe Ross Murray and those of us with downtown businesses, we locals live with an open door policy. You need something? Come on in. So Mimi's request was not the least bit odd. Really.

When I arrived at Mimi's house, her dachshund triplets, Oscar, Meyer and Frank, greeted me at her door. They spilled over each other in a writhing mass of stubby legs and elongated bellies, desperate for affection. As far as they were concerned, there was never enough love to go around. I took my time playing with the dogs, significantly depleting Mimi's stash of dog biscuits during their favorite game, Catch the Cookie. After all, there was no rush. Edna wouldn't be awake for hours.

I kicked off my shoes by the back door and padded to Mimi's room at the side of the house. On the way by, I poked my nose in Mike's home office. It seemed the handheld GPS he'd taken on his treasure hunt was no longer a secret. It sat on the computer desk between the laser mouse and an mp3 player. I was tempted to pause a moment and listen to a tune, but Mike loved Country, and well, let's just say I didn't.

Mimi's room contained stacks of Celtic CD's neatly shelved beside her CD player. Apart from the table lamps, her CD player was the only electric appliance in the room. I found the jar of cream where Mimi said, and the little blue and white gift bags in the cupboard, but her business card holder was empty.

Hmmm. I tugged my ponytail as I surveyed the room, trying to decide where Mimi might keep her cards. They weren't shelved beside the gift bags or the tissue wrap or the empty jars. They weren't stowed with the stationary or Mimi's boxed supply of paperclips and felt-tipped pens. They weren't in the wooden box containing her special recipes for facial masks and herbal potions, or in the Rolodex file that recorded her clients and what sorts of things they used.

My hand hovered over the Rolodex, fingers trembling like a witching stick over water. Dare I peek?

Instead I checked Mimi's desk drawers. Since she'd told me to include her card in Edna's package I felt justified snooping. But Mimi's Rolodex?

Gosh it was tempting and really who'd ever know, besides Oscar, Meyer and Frank?

I remembered the week Doc announced his retirement. I'd come back early from lunch and discovered Doc and Mimi arguing in his office. The two were so hard at it, neither noticed me trying not to listen.

Doc accused Mimi of some kind of unethical practice, but Mimi wasn't backing down. At least not until Doc threatened to expose her.

"You're playing a dangerous game," Doc said. "And I can't effectively treat Mike until you stop."

"What I give my husband is completely harmless."

"If it's so harmless, why do you sneak it into his food? Why not tell him up front what you're doing to him?"

"You know perfectly well why I can't tell him."

"Mimi, you have to stop this immediately or I'll tell Mike myself. I can't keep this a secret."

"You break my confidence and you'll regret it. Sasha and Sam aren't the only ones who can bring charges against you."

"I've done nothing illegal."

"You'll be broke before you can prove that, though." The door slammed on her way out.

OK, maybe Mimi hadn't backed down.

I glanced down her hallway, making sure no one was about, and flipped on Mimi's desk light. It seemed I just couldn't resist browsing through her Rolodex and really, what harm was there?

I found Mike's card in her rotary file and, using a sticky note I found in her desk drawer, I copied what she'd recorded. *Vitex agnus-castus*. The Latin wasn't much help so I tried looking it up in one of her reference books. I could find *Vitex*-this and *Vitex*-that but not the kind Mimi was apparently giving her husband.

Back in Mike's office, I used his computer to search for *Vitex agnus-castus*. According to the articles I found, the plant was traditionally called Chaste Tree and was used to treat PMS and other female complaints. It stimulated progesterone production. Even I knew men didn't need progesterone. Why would she give it to Mike?

I was rereading the article when Geoff Grant filled the doorway, his frown deepening the clefts in his cheeks. "If you think Mike is mixed up in Doc's death why risk snooping around in his house?"

Seeing him face to face for the first time since I made an idiot of myself the night before, proved awkward. My cheeks flushed warm and I hoped he interpreted my embarrassment as guilt for being caught.

"I'm not snooping. I'm running an errand for Mimi."

He folded his arms across his chest. "I know. She

sent me to tell you where she put her new business cards. They're not in Mike's office, by the way."

The dogs, who should have been barking, lay stomach up at his feet. Obviously, he'd been rubbing them for a while before he spoke. Little traitors.

"Since you're here, come look at this and tell me what it means," I invited.

He stepped up behind me and read. "I think it's pretty self-explanatory."

"But why give this stuff to Mike?"

"Mimi gave this to Mike? That doesn't make sense. Does he have prostate cancer?"

"Not that I ever heard of."

"Then there's no reason. You must have misinterpreted something"

"A couple weeks ago I overheard Mimi and Doc arguing. They were threatening each other. I wanted to know if it was connected to what's been happening. Besides, Mimi has access to your apartment. She could sneak up and stick poison in the tuna you feed Sheba."

"You honestly think your cousin would hurt your cat?"

"Sheba'd never take food from a stranger."

He dug his fists into his pockets. "So it's Mimi or me. Is that why you were crying last night?"

"No." Lori's late night question came to mind, though. Was I afraid Geoff might be involved in Doc's murder? Should I be? "I don't know. Maybe. You've said things."

"What kind of things?"

"You've hinted at some shameful secret, something terrible that happened to you in Africa. And you have all those poison books. I know it's hateful for me to even think it, but nothing bad happened in Hum

Harbour before you moved home. It was quiet and peaceful and everyone was happy—"

"If Hum Harbour's truly the Eden you imagine, how come Sam's cheating on my sister, Ross Murray is gambling away his fortune, Mimi's doping her husband and Bud Fisher is drinking himself into a stupor? You know, Gailynn, you never mention Bud when you're dealing out suspects."

"Because he's Lori's dad."

"So he automatically gets a free pass?"

"I don't want him to be involved."

"But it's OK if I am?"

I didn't answer.

Geoff reached over my shoulder and hit sleep on the computer's keyboard. The screen went dark.

"Let's go for a walk," Geoff said. "There are some things I need to tell you."

25

"I'd like to go someplace quiet where we won't be bothered," Geoff said.

"The cemetery? No one will be there until this afternoon."

So that's where we went.

In Hum Harbour, the cemetery's the end of the road both figuratively and literally. It's been the final resting place for local residents for over two hundred years, which is about as old as it gets by Canadian standards. There's a section where the grave markers are so lichen-covered they're indecipherable. And when the fog rolls in and the waves smash against the rocks below, it feels like you've been transported to another world, another time.

That morning the sky was heavy. Dark rain clouds clung to the hills, trailing misty fingers down the steep slopes. The cemetery's grass was neon green, fresh cut and fragrant in preparation for Doc's interment. We could see the pile of dark earth that marked his waiting grave. In case there were more preparations necessary, we strolled to the far end of the graveyard where a stone bench sits under a weather-twisted evergreen. The bench is made from the ballast stones of the HMS Humphrey, the boat that carried the original settlers to Hum Harbour back in 1779. The bench was wet but Geoff spread his jacket and we sat on it.

"It'll take me a while to get used to all this green," he said. "Somalia was so brown. Dry, dusty earth, never enough water. I'd imagined coming home would be like stepping into a garden and it is in a way. I just forgot about the snakes. I thought I'd left them all in Africa."

I didn't interrupt.

"Have you ever heard anyone tell you, you can't run away from your problems? They follow you wherever you go? Maybe not you. You don't run away from things."

"You do?"

He shrugged. "I think I can say in all honesty that moving to Africa was as much about avoiding Hum Harbour as it was about following God's call. I wanted to escape. Our parents were dead, Sasha happily married—or so I thought—nothing to keep me in Nova Scotia."

"It wasn't God's call?"

"Yes, it was. But His call meant my freedom, at least that's what I used to think." He clasped his hands between his knees. "How much do you know about Somalia's politics?"

"There's a civil war and millions of people are homeless. And there are these guys that ride horses and raid the refugee camps. I saw something about them on the news once."

He nodded. "They steal young boys and turn them into warriors. They execute the men they consider dangerous. They rape the women."

"Is there nothing anyone can do?"

"We tried, but it was clear we'd never succeed. All we could do was offer medical help."

"How many of you were there?"

"At our camp? Seven doctors, a dozen nurses. We came from around the world, different backgrounds, different languages, one hope. I grew especially close to one man, Amado, a Spanish priest. He truly lived the scripture 'faith without works is dead."

"Is he still there?"

Geoff stared at the swirling cove below. "Do you remember what I told you about trust?"

I nodded.

"We'd made a truce with the local officials. We'd care for any wounded who came our way and in turn they would protect us from the various militias working in our area. Despite the government's promise, though, we received no protection."

I waited.

"No matter when a shipment of medical supplies was due, the militias found out. They'd ride through the camp, stampeding the tents, firing their guns in the air, and in the midst of the confusion they'd steal whatever they could. Amado believed someone was informing the militias, so he came up with a plan to deliver our next shipment of antibiotics and morphine ahead of schedule. Then we'd hide them in an abandoned well. We needed the drugs desperately and we thought our scheme would work."

Geoff plucked a blade of grass and folded in half and half again.

"Instead of slipping into camp quietly, like Amado had arranged, the trucks arrived with a flashy government escort. They couldn't have garnered more attention if they set off fireworks. Before we could even start unloading the trucks, we were attacked. Total chaos."

I pressed my hands to my mouth.

"Several people were caught in the crossfire, including Amado. I told myself he was hit by a stray bullet, but the others thought he'd been targeted. You see, selling our supplies on the black market could raise millions. Everyone from the informants to the raiders would get a cut of the profits. Amado was bad for business."

I touched the back of his hand. "Geoff, I'm so sorry."

"Miraculously Amado wasn't killed. He was med-evaced back to Spain and I went along, stayed with him in Barcelona until he started rehab."

His eyes seemed a darker blue than usual, their color as tumultuous as the waves below. "Then I came home. Doc's offer to sell me the practice was God-sent and I grabbed onto it with both hands. But as much as I wanted to come home to Hum Harbour, Gailynn, I didn't kill Doc for his practice. I'm too much of a coward to harm anyone."

Unable to hold his gaze I stared at our hands.

"Now you know."

I didn't believe for a minute that Geoff Grant was a coward, but I couldn't think of anything to say that wouldn't be glib or insulting. So for once in my life, I had the wisdom to hold my tongue. God was answering my prayer after all, just in a way I didn't expect.

Geoff slowly turned his hand over and I threaded my fingers between his. We watched the rain on the grass.

Bud Fisher drove by on the dirt track above the cemetery. His old diesel pickup made so much noise it drowned out the whoosh of the waves pounding the shore below us. He threw something out the driver's side window and kept going. A crow flew down from an evergreen to check what Bud had tossed. Apparently it was nothing interesting because he flew back to his shelter empty-handed. Or was that empty beaked?

26

It was hard to believe one week ago Doc was happily sailing towards his Caribbean retirement. Sitting in the pew at Third Church, watching people file up to the front and pay their last respects to Doc Campbell in his open casket, I thought cliché thoughts about the frailty of life and the unexpectedness of death. If ever anyone understood that, it was Geoff.

For five years Geoff had battled man's darkest side—sickness, greed, corruption—until he could bear it no more. He came home hoping to exchange the Somalian camp's misery for green grass and good old Canadian goodness. Instead, he was once again face-to-face with man's sinfulness at its extreme. Someone had murdered Doc Campbell. What was more wicked than that?

The church was already crowded when I arrived and I found a vacant spot near the back. Geoff sat directly behind me. I could feel his gaze branding my neck.

When he first told me his secret, I'd been overwhelmed. I knew I had to be sympathetic. I couldn't walk away. But since then I'd been struggling to decide how I should react to him. Acting like nothing between us had changed, which was what I'd been going for, didn't seem to be working. People kept glancing at me as though I had some kind of sign emblazoned on my forehead. Maybe if I could have read the sign I'd have had a better handle on my emotions.

Bud walked down the aisle. He was clean-shaven, his curling grey hair neatly combed. He wore his funeral suit and dark tie. He hadn't looked this neat since Ellen's memorial service.

Lori's hand rested on his arm. Immaculate in the form fitting black suit, she looked equally funereal. She nodded, a fleeting pucker between her beautifully arched brows. No doubt she remembered my panicked phone call at one in the morning and attributed my rebar-stiff spine to that.

If I seemed confused then, how would I describe what I was feeling now?

Was I angry about what Geoff had told me? Yes. How could people do the vile things he described, and live with themselves? Was I frightened? Definitely. If evil could triumph in Somalia, why not in Canada? In Hum Harbour? Who was going to stop it?

Someone famous, I can't remember who, once said that for evil to triumph, all you need is for good people to do nothing. Would I be one of those good people who sat on their hands while evil ran rampant in the streets of Hum Harbour? Should I sit silently in my pew and risk my village's future? My heart pounded against my ribs. There was more than a golf course at stake here, and I, for one, thought ensuring the peace and security of my village was worth any risk I had to take.

Blissfully unaware of the riot of emotions bouncing around inside of me, Ross and Rickie Murray nodded their greeting as they followed Lori down the aisle. They also wore black, although their clothes

ned haute couture, Ross keeping the myth of hi
ss wealth alive. I noticed when they paused t
Rickie's vase of white orchids, his fists
d. Was it grief at his friend's passing, the price
se, or memories of a glass-smashing spree at
ass that moved him?

were flowers everywhere. I'm no big fan of
they seemed to be the blossom of choice.
hids stood out like pearls among pebbles.
vore a navy flowered dress with a lace
his gray suit. Mike owned two suits and
em. Tomorrow he'd wear the navy pin
h. They walked hand in hand, to all the
y couple. Who'd imagine pleasantly
vas doping her husband with women's
hy?

nmotion ensued at the back of the
riveled in my seat. Vi Murray, in
was greeting Marjorie Campbell
lost sister and Ross Murray's first
Marjorie since she taught me in
kid. Her long face looked sterner
naybe that had more to do with
anything else. She endured it
course everyone was watching,
e'd react towards the woman

cleft chin and showed a stiff
elf, probably escaping to the
ossible moment.

wedged himself into the
is rusty eyebrows shot up as
iff posture. "You OK?"
question. "I know Doc

Campbell wasn't the greatest physician in the world, but he was our Doc and I loved him. He brought most of us here into the world and it's like we've lost a piece of ourselves, of our history. I feel hollow."

"We'll find who did it."

He withdrew a folded piece of paper from his suit inside pocket. Sliding his arm along the pew back behind me, he turned to Geoff. "I need to talk to you after the funeral. Have a look at this and tell me wha you think?"

"What was that?" I asked.

"Lab results just came in. I need Geoff to deciph them for me."

"From Doc's autopsy? That's fast, isn't it?"

"Yeah. From what I hear, the provincial usually sits on stuff for months. If this is proof Doc murdered, we could very well have his killer locked before the end of the week."

A shiver skidded down my spine. The killer here, among us. One of these good people whon known all my life was a murderer. I knew it, I knew I was the only black haired MacDonald in generations or that I was losing my heart to Grant, the man sitting in the pew behind Unwelcome, unwanted truths I could not escape.

"What does the report say?"

"It's all gobbledygook as far as I'm con That's why I need Geoff to translate."

The church was crammed full of mourners service was ready to begin. Sam and Sasha appeared. I presume they thought by timi arrival to the last possible moment they'd av of the whispers. However, seeing as the onl seats were at the front of the church, everyone's attention as they walked up the aisle.

Sam looked rumpled. His suit was too tight so he left the jacket unbuttoned and his tie, knotted too short, rested like a bib on his prominent tummy. Sasha wore her navy blue pantsuit. It drained the color from her already pale face, and she'd compensated by adding her violet earrings and a bright fuchsia scarf. As they settled into their seats in the front pew, Sasha's scarf seemed to snag every gaze in the room and everybody had something to say about it. I, however, couldn't keep my eyes off her seaglass earrings. She'd found the second one.

Before I could scoot up to her, Andrew placed his hand on my knee and pressed. "Sit still," he mouthed.

I mutinously obeyed.

Doc's only surviving relative, Marjorie Campbell Murray, took her place and Reverend Innes began the service.

I regret to confess I did not listen. Instead, I studied the congregation, wondering for the zillionth time, who could Doc's murderer be? I adamantly refused to believe Sasha was involved, but did it therefore follow Doc's killer had to be a man? A woman could administer poison as easily as any man. Maybe easier, since who would suspect her of foul intentions? The more I thought the more my gaze slid back to my cousin's fuzzy red hair. Who in Hum Harbour was more versed in poisons than my cousin Mimi? Who was more trusted? Who was more devious? I was sure Mike had no idea his wife was poisoning him.

All right, a progesterone stimulant wasn't poison, but it could never be considered natural.

My thoughts careened downhill from there. Mimi

had access to Sheba's food. It would be a snap for her to poison my cat. No doubt she ordered her poison through Sasha, which made Sasha the ideal scapegoat. After all, Mimi was very familiar with Sasha's vulnerabilities. And when I'd overheard Doc accuse Mimi of unethical conduct Mimi had threatened him back. She was not acting like my favorite, mild-mannered cousin then, that's for sure.

The more I thought about it and the more I studied her, the more convinced I became. More than anyone else here, Mimi had motive and the means to poison Doc. In fact—the idea dawned on me in a eureka flash-bulb moment—she also had the perfect opportunity with that coconut cream pie she made for Doc's retirement party. Mimi had insisted the pie was for Doc alone. No one else was allowed a bite.

And I'd forced him to take that second slice!

Could Doc's murderer really be Mimi, with me as her unwitting accomplice?

I snapped out of my trance as Reverend Innes lifted his arms to pronounce the benediction.

27

The funeral procession wound through Hum Harbour. I later heard there were so many cars the entire length of town was clogged with our slow moving vehicles. I drove with Andrew and Geoff, slumped in the back seat of the police cruiser. Another time I might have had fun stuffing things through the grating just to irritate my older brother. Today I was too overcome with grief.

Mimi, the woman I'd known my whole life, the one who'd encouraged me to start my own business, the woman who babysat me when I was young and whose kids I sometimes watched over even now, was a murderer.

Andrew and Geoff were too busy talking in the front seat to notice the shudders that wracked me. I buttoned my jacket up to my chin and tapped on the wire grating.

"Let me out," I said. "I'll walk from here."

"It's drizzling," said Andrew.

"Scottish mist."

The hearse was parked along the path closest to the open grave. Its back stood open as the McKennas maneuvered Doc's shiny oak coffin out of the car and over to the open ground. Dale nodded his absent-minded greeting. Beyond him, I could see Mimi and Mike talking with Ross and Rickie.

I hovered on the edge of the crowd watching Mimi, convinced she was Doc's killer, yet unable to believe it was true.

Andrew appeared beside me. Unlike Sam, who seldom thought about anything or anyone besides Sam, Andrew could always tell when I was upset. He wasn't necessarily good at figuring out what was wrong, but he always noticed.

"Hang in there, kid," he said. "Doc would hate you crying over him."

"It's not that." I pushed unhappily at my damp hair, which hung limp and heavy down my back. "I need to tell you something. In confidence. You have to promise you won't say it was me who told you."

Maybe he felt sorry for me, maybe I piqued his curiosity. Whatever his reasons Andrew didn't brush me off. Instead he nabbed my elbow and led me a few feet from the crowd.

"OK, what's so important it can't wait?"

I swallowed my doubts and whispered, "It's Mimi," as if whispering made my accusation less horrible.

"What's Mimi?"

"Doc's murderer. He was going to blow the whistle on Mimi, tell Mike what she was doing and she couldn't allow that to happen so she..." I glanced across the grass to where my cousin stood. She looked right into my eyes, and that's when I knew for certain. And I knew she knew I knew.

"She killed Doc."

Andrew's eyes widened. "Mimi? Are you crazy?"

"Shush! Not so loud. She'll hear."

"You can't be serious, Gai."

"But it fits. And when I started asking questions

about Doc, she even poisoned my cat."

"Mimi would never poison an animal."

"She didn't mean for it to be deadly, just to make Sheba sick. She only meant to scare me, but I stayed out longer than normal and Sheba almost died."

Andrew set his arm around my shoulders and tried to lead me away. "Gailynn, Gailynn," he said. "You're overwrought." He used his professional, soothing cop tone, the one guaranteed to calm the most agitated perps.

I shook myself free. "Overwrought? Of course I am. Who wouldn't be?"

Lori was beside me, now. "Gai, hush, it's all right."

I made the effort to drop my voice. "No it's not all right. Why are you people so blind? Mimi killed Doc because he knew her secret."

"What secret?" demanded Mike, suddenly appearing behind Lori.

I stared at him in horror, or was it shame? He wasn't supposed to hear this from me. It was supposed to be Andrew telling him about Mimi's duplicity. Not me.

Why, oh why hadn't I taken Andrew's lead and let him drag me away? My cheeks felt like fire and I pressed my cold palms against them.

"Nothing, never mind," I said. I tried to escape, but my cousin's husband blocked my path.

"What secret, Gailynn?" Mike asked again.

The drizzle had thickened to steady rain, chilling me to my bones. I shrank into my jacket, praying the earth would swallow me.

Instead, Andrew put on his official face and ordered, "Tell him, Gailynn. Tell us all."

By now, 'all' included Mimi, and she looked so

innocent I almost backed down. Except I couldn't. Doc deserved justice. I loved him, and I loved Mike, and I loved Mimi too. I had to stop her before she hurt anyone else. So I sucked in a deep breath and squared my shoulders and said, "Mike, Mimi's poisoning your food."

Mimi's cheeks flushed a brilliant red. "It's not poison."

"You don't deny it?"

Her auburn curls bristled. "Of course I deny poisoning my husband."

Andrew just shook his head sadly. "Gailynn, stop before you say anything else you're going to regret."

"Or what? Mimi'll shut me up by poisoning me, too?"

Mimi's bosom swelled with apparent indignation. "I am not poisoning my husband. I give him herbal supplements."

"Then why not tell him?"

Mimi's hazel eyes flashed and she folded her arms across her chest, as though trying to hold in her anger. "This is extremely embarrassing, Gailynn. Must we air my dirty laundry in front of half the town?"

Lori said, "If there's nothing wrong with what you've been doing why not tell us?"

I could have hugged Lori for standing up for me like that. I could tell by the concern in her lovely violet eyes she thought I was just as crazy as everyone else thought, but she was my friend and she supported me anyway.

Mike shifted closer. "What're they talking about, Mimi? Tell me."

"It's about those herbs I give you. Gailynn's found out."

Mike groaned skyward. "And now she's blabbing this to everyone? Gailynn, why can't you ever keep your nose out of other people's business?"

Lori's beautiful eyebrows rose. "Your own wife is poisoning you and you want Gailynn to keep quiet about it?"

I nodded, encouraged. Perhaps Lori did believe me after all.

Mike stood close to his wife. "That's right. It's none of your business. Any of you."

"But she poisoned Doc, too!" I practically shouted.

Mimi gripped my arm. "Gailynn, a lot of people have my medicinals in their cupboards, even you. Anyone could have poisoned Doc."

"But you were the one sneaking stuff into Mike's food. Doc found out, and he told you to stop, and you threatened him. I heard you with my own ears."

Andrew shifted closer. "Is that true, Mimi?"

"That I threatened Doc? Of course not. I might have told him people in glass houses shouldn't throw stones but I never threatened to kill him."

"And the stuff you're giving Mike?" Andrew asked.

"Oh, for heaven's sake, must I?"

"Is it poison?"

"Of course not. It was an anti-aphrodisiac."

"A what?" I said.

"An anti-aphrodisiac. It was to reduce Mike's—" she hesitated, "libido."

Mike stared at his feet.

"It worked so well on the boys I thought if it keeps Oscar, Meyer and Frank from straying, maybe it would keep Mike home more."

"You mean it's the same the same stuff you feed

the dogs?" Andrew sounded incredulous. Well, so was I.

"I've seen the results of a faithless husband and I didn't want to end up out on my ear like Vi, or despondent like poor Sasha."

"So you took matters into your own hands, is that what you're saying, Mimi?"

She nodded. "Gailynn, I cannot believe you would humiliate me like this."

Andrew elbowed me in the ribs and I glared at him, unable to come up with an adequate response.

"I apologize on my sister's behalf," he said. "And I will take her home before she does anything worse."

He dragged me away.

I wasn't ready to give up, though. "That's it? You're going to let her go? How do you know she didn't poison Doc, anyway? How can you believe her?"

"Because Geoff told me what did kill Doc. It was methanol. Plain old wood alcohol and anyone with half a brain coulda stuck it in Doc's whiskey. Mimi, as you've already pointed out, would have been a lot more imaginative."

28

Have you ever been so humiliated you wanted to crawl into a hole and die? It wasn't the first time I'd been an idiot and it wouldn't be the last, but some days I even horrified myself. At least people no longer whispered about Sam and Sasha, although under the circumstances that was little comfort.

Obviously I did not attend the post funeral luncheon in the church basement. Instead I took my office keys and let myself into the clinic. I still wasn't convinced Mimi'd told all, although what could be more embarrassing than publicly admitting you were emasculating your husband, I didn't know.

I shamelessly read Mike's medical file through from beginning to end. There were the usual childhood ailments, sports injuries in high school and the gall bladder attacks ten years ago. I remembered his attacks inspired Mimi to investigate herbal medicines in the first place.

Mike's most recent medical appointments centered on male complaints. According to Doc's notes, Mike had been helping himself to something called betel nut. Apparently, Mimi kept it on hand for cancer treatment and Mike discovered it also had other properties. Problem was the betel nut did not cure Mike's condition so he began taking more and more that, unfortunately, lead to some rather unpleasant side effects. Doc convinced Mike to stop self-medicating and treated his side effects, which gave Mike some relief but did nothing for his original complaint.

That's when Doc decided a family conference was in order and invited Mimi to one of Mike's appointments. He discovered Mimi was feeding Mike *vitex agnus-castus*, better known as Chaste Tree. Apparently, the more Mike had tried to fix his condition, the more Chaste Tree she fed him.

Doc confronted Mimi—no doubt the argument I overheard—and insisted she stop doping Mike immediately. I gathered from Doc's last notation, despite her fury, Mimi had complied. Or at least Mike stopped complaining.

I stuffed Mike's file back into the cabinet. That might have been the end of his problem, but nothing in Mike's chart hinted at Doc's glass house, as Mimi put it. Now what?

I thought and thought until I remembered my conversation with Vi the other afternoon at the church office.

"Go through Doc's old medical files and look up Jack Murray's cause of death," she'd told me. "If it's kosher then I haven't said anything slanderous," which implied Jack Murray's death was anything but.

The old files were kept in the same room but in a different filing cabinet than the active files. I rolled open the M drawer and fingered my way to Murray, Jack Charles. It was a thick folder. He'd been an old man with a history of poor health.

At that moment, as I held Jack Murray's weighty file in my hand, I almost backed down. I almost conceded tracking Doc's murderer was better left to Andrew and his police cronies. I almost gave up the fight.

Then I remembered Doc lying motionless on the Medical Convention's deck. I remembered Sheba's limp body, like a black ink stain on the clinic's paper-covered bed, and I remembered the blood red shards of shattered glass smeared across the floor of Dunmaglass, and I got mad. Fury boiled up with the bile at the back of my throat.

No one was going to hurt the people I loved without being held accountable. No one was going to get away with secrets. Whoever did these crimes must be stopped. Now. Before they killed again. And if I had to endure shame and humiliation to see the truth come out, well, so be it.

I'd apologize to Mimi and Mike for my shameful conduct, but I wasn't backing down.

I would find Doc's killer or die trying.

I slammed Jack Murray's file onto the top of the filing cabinet and flipped open the cover. This was where I'd look next.

I figured Jack's early years weren't relevant so I concentrated on his later illnesses. He'd been hospitalized repeatedly for congestive heart failure, liver sclerosis, high blood pressure and gout. Final cause of death was heart failure resulting from a cerebral hemorrhage, or stroke. It sounded natural enough to me, I mean, how could Ross induce a stroke? If that was what Vi implied Ross had done.

I took the page listing Jack Murray's medications to Geoff's office and started checking them against his giant pharmacology text that details every drug on the face of the earth. I was reading the precautions under the eighth pill listed when Geoff stuck his nose in, scaring me half out of my skin.

"What are you doing?"

"Checking Jack Murray's meds from the time he died."

"And why are you doing that?"

"Because Vi suggested Jack's death might be questionable. If that's the case and Doc knew Ross was involved, Ross had a reason to silence Doc."

"Gailynn, put the file away."

I shook my head. "This afternoon I made a complete fool of myself in front of every last person in Hum Harbour. I admit it. I need to redeem myself."

"Leave crime solving to the police, Gailynn."

"There's a murderer running around Hum Harbour and we have to help stop him. Otherwise, if we don't, we're no better than those corrupt people in Somalia."

Geoff folded his arms across his chest. "How do you figure that?"

"You said they didn't stand against evil."

"So snooping in people's confidential medical files is your idea of combating evil?"

"You told me I could look through Doc's files."

"That's when you were searching for his golf course contract. I didn't sanction your violating patient confidentiality."

"It's not like I'm going to blab what I learn all over town," I said. "I'm simply looking for avenues of investigation."

His frown weakened ever so slightly, so I rushed on. "For example, come look at this. Is there any way Ross Murray could have triggered his father's fatal stroke? These are the meds the old man was on. What do you think?"

I could see him wavering, determined to stand

firm, yet unquestionably curious. What could Jack Murray's meds have to do with Doc Campbell's murder? He rounded the desk. "This discussion isn't over, you know."

"I know. But couldn't you just look at this file? Please?"

As Geoff read, I closed my eyes and thanked the Lord for this small reprieve. "There's nothing untoward here, Gailynn."

Geoff's distinctive scent filled my nostrils. It was unlike anything else I knew. "You're sure?"

"I'm the doctor, remember?"

I chewed the inside of my cheek. "What else could Mimi have meant when she threatened Doc?"

"Maybe you misunderstood, Gailynn. Maybe she was warning not threatening."

"Believe me, I've heard Mimi warn and I've heard her threaten and I can tell the difference."

"So, now you want to go through every file in this office to see if you can find something?"

"Not every file," I said. "But with your permission, I'd like to check the ones I think might include motives for silencing Doc."

"I thought the point of your snooping was to discover the motive. How do you know ahead of time who's harboring a secret?"

"If there is one thing I'm learning in all this, it's that everyone has a secret. No one is what they appear to be on the outside."

"My point, exactly. You'll need to review every file."

"I've already checked as far as C, although I wasn't actually hunting for patients' secrets at that point, so I guess you're right. If I'm going to do this

He began rolling up his sleeves. Was he going to help me search? "Did you ever find a copy of the Hum Harbour Holes agreement?"

I shook my head. "Nor anything pertaining to the sale of Doc's medical practice."

"I get your interest in the Holes, but why Doc's practice?"

I waved a dismissive hand. "Just something Lori said once. Made me curious."

He leaned against the desk. "What did she say?"

"I really can't remember." I adjusted the pages in Jack Murray's file and closed it.

"Anyone ever tell you you're a terrible liar?"

"Too often. But I'm still not going to tell you what I wanted to know because it doesn't matter anymore."

"You're sure?"

I met his gaze. "I'm sure."

He pinched the bridge of his nose. "I assume you'd already checked Mike Johnson's file before you accused him and Mimi. Have you looked into Ross or Bud, the other investors?"

"No, Ross's dad, but not Ross himself."

Geoff studied me for a full minute then seemed to come to a decision. "This goes against my better judgment, but let's make a deal. We go through the files together. We find anything we take it straight to Andrew. But if we find nothing you'll stop your private investigation."

Stop completely? "You would search with me?" I asked.

"Gailynn, if it's what I need to do to save you from another disaster like the one this afternoon, I'd review these files from now 'til doomsday."

I eased back in his chair. "You're concerned someone might sue you?"

"That's part of it," he admitted.

"You've other reasons? What?"

He almost smiled. "Lets give it a little longer. See which mystery you crack first."

29

Geoff sat on one side of his desk and I sat on the other. We read through Ross and Bud's medical files silently. Geoff read faster than I did, and I felt a little intimidated by the speed with which he devoured each page before flipping to the next. Fortunately, Ross's file was longer than Bud's, which I was reading, so I didn't feel like I was falling too far behind.

I scanned each page first then went back and read more closely to make sure I didn't miss something important. Geoff had challenged me not to let my prejudices blind me. Being Lori's dad was not reason enough to exclude Bud from my suspicions. So I wanted to be sure I scrutinized his records with as much care as I would anyone else's.

"Anything interesting?" I asked when Geoff reached for a book on his shelf.

"Yeah. I think Doc might have overlooked something. There's been research in the last few years that suggests a correlation between certain types of liver cancers and their frequency within a given population group."

A tiny pucker formed between his eyebrows as he warmed to his subject. "You see, until recently the connection's been attributed to nutritional-environmental factors, but researchers now believe they may have uncovered a genetic marker which, if identified early enough, could substantially influence the disease's early diagnosis and treatment. I see here from Doc's records that Ross suffers from the same—you don't care about this do you?"

"Would it give Ross a good reason to murder Doc?"

"No. But I think I'll have you call Ross early next week and set up an appointment. I'd like to discuss this with him."

I scribbled a note to myself on Geoff's memo pad. "You know, if this is going to mean I end up booking appointments for every person who has a file in there"—meaning the filing cabinets filling the next room—"it's going to take us forever to do this."

Sheepishly Geoff slid his reference book back on the shelf and flipped to the last page in Ross's records. "I think I'll have a look through Ross Junior's file, too. It wouldn't be the first time a parent did something illegal to protect their child."

"So you think it's Ross?"

"Just saying it's worth checking."

Humphing, I returned to the pages before me. I was stumped by some of the older lab sheets in Bud's folder. The forms were laid out differently than the ones I was used to filing and the scales they used to measure results seemed completely screwy.

"Can you explain this to me?" I raised my voice so Geoff could hear me in the next room. "I can't make heads or tails out of these test results when I compare them with the newer requisitions at the back of Bud's file."

"Aha, you've been bitten by the curiosity bug, too. What mysterious ailments lurk in peoples' pasts?"

"OK, you caught me, but can you tell me what this

means?"

He settled into his seat, feet propped on the other empty chair, and stretched out his hand. "Sure, pass it over."

I rested my chin on my hands and watched him read.

Frowning, he read the front, then the back of the old lab report, and the front again. "Where'd you find this?"

He came around the desk and shuffled through the pages of Bud's chart. "Here, you read Ross Junior's, and let me look through Bud's more thoroughly."

We exchanged files and I half turned my attention to my new file. I already knew most of what it contained since I'd worked at the clinic for most of Ross Junior's life. I read fitfully. I wouldn't have recognized the liver symptoms Geoff seemed so keen on even if I'd been attentive.

"What's wrong with Bud?" I finally asked. "You keep going back to that one set of tests. Is he all right?"

"What? Bud? Yeah, sure." Geoff took Bud's papers to the file room.

I followed. "Come on, if nothing's wrong what's so interesting, then?"

"Lori's Mom worked for Doc when you were kids, right?"

"Yeah. Lori practically grew up in this clinic. From the time we started kindergarten, she either came here or my place every day after school. Why?"

"And Bud got along with Doc?"

"Sure. I guess. Why? Are you reading Lori's file now?"

"Can you find me Ellen's in the retired files, please?"

I pulled it out and handed it to him. "Are you going to tell me what this is about?"

It seemed he found what he was looking for because he handed Ellen's file back to me after briefly scanning two pages. He replaced Lori's file, as well.

"We need to talk about confidentiality."

"Again? I've already promised I won't mention what I learn here."

"No, right now I'm thinking about how the things we discover might affect you personally."

30

My knees felt weak and I sank into the closest chair. My brain ran amok with lab results and Geoff's remarks about genetic markers and kinds of cancers that ran in families. "What are you saying? Lori's sick? She's got the same cancer her Mom did?"

He pulled the other chair close and sat. Resting his elbows on his thighs, he clasped and unclasped his hands. "Lori's fine."

"Her dad?"

"Bud's fine, too. Look there's no polite way to say this and it's too late to convince you it's nothing, but I'm not sure it necessarily has anything to do with Doc. OK?"

"What is it?"

"Those test results you didn't understand? They indicate Bud was, shall we say, unable to father children." He waited for me to catch up.

"You're saying that Lori...that's impossible."

He shrugged. "Apparently not."

"Lori's adopted?"

"Ellen Fisher gave birth to a live baby girl the same year you were born so, no, Lori is not adopted." He let that sink in.

"Do you think they know? Lori and Bud?"

"You tell me."

I tugged my hair. If Lori knew she would have

told me, especially when I went through the phase where I thought I was adopted. No, Lori didn't know, but did Bud?

"Who could her father be, then?"

Geoff still said nothing.

Whoever he was, the man most likely lived in Hum Harbour, or had at one time. I pictured my friend's lovely face. Lori had her Mom's blonde hair and violet eyes. Her perfectly shaped brows were too sculpted to say whose they were like and her dimpled chin, well, who did I know with a dimpled chin?

I let the faces I'd seen at Doc's funeral parade through my mind, but I couldn't picture one man with a dimpled or cleft chin. My brothers were both the spitting images of our dad, no dimples. Mike Johnson passed his block features onto his sons, too. Vi's genes moderated Ross Murray's, so although young RJ's jaw wasn't as soft as his Dad's, the family likeness remained unmistakable. Ross's second wife reminded me of Marjorie Campbell, his first wife. Vi's perkiness contrasted starkly to Marjorie's lean, athletic build.

Marjorie Campbell had a cleft chin. And so did her brother.

"No."

Geoff must have read it all in my face. "Think about it," he said. "Ellen worked for Doc from before Lori was born. It's possible that she and Doc developed feelings for each other. That they acted on those feelings at least once."

"No."

"Why not?"

"Because she couldn't. She wouldn't. Maybe Ellen wasn't much of a church goer but she'd never have done anything to hurt her family. Especially Lori. She loved Lori."

"But before Lori, couldn't she have had an affair with Doc before she had Lori?"

How would I know? I tried to picture young Bud Fisher, the lobster fisherman, and compare him to Douglas Campbell, Hum Harbour's handsome, charming doctor. It wasn't hard to imagine any woman finding Doc more appealing than taciturn Bud Fisher. But Bud's wife?

"OK, say it's true and Bud knew. Why would he join a business arrangement with his wife's ex-lover? Hmm?"

Geoff shook his head.

"And why wait over twenty-five years before retaliating?"

"I haven't got an answer."

"Why not just watch Doc sail off to the Caribbean, and be thankful to be rid of him?"

"Gailynn, I don't know."

"Why murder him, now?"

"OK, you're right. It doesn't make sense. Let's forget I even mentioned it."

But of course, I couldn't.

****

After reviewing Ross and Bud's medical files, we agreed to stop for dinner; this seemed the ideal time to take a break. Geoff offered to make his internationally renowned ragout while I checked Sheba. I accepted.

Four hours earlier I'd left an uncharacteristically dopey cat snoozing on the middle of my bed. Sheba was due some serious love and affection.

Cats are independent creatures and Sheba could

be called Feline Poster Cat of the Decade. I discovered her fully revived, sitting on the windowsill watching a robin saunter along the deck rail. Sheba's tail twitched.

"Sure you're up to this?" I asked, carefully lifting her into my arms.

She rubbed her head under my chin.

"You've been through a lot. Maybe you should take it easy for another day or two." I unlatched the sliding door. The rain was over but there were still puddles on my deck. "What do you think?" I asked and pushed the door wide.

She exploded from my arms. Logic tells me her paws touched the deck before she pounced onto the rail a breath of a second behind the airborne bird, but I didn't see it. With the agility of an Olympic gymnast, she strutted the thin edge of the rail, dismounted on Geoff's side and escaped down his back stair.

Well, so much for love and affection.

I watched her slink under Geoff's car, scoot across Water Street and disappear between the trucks parked near the wharf. Guess she was feeling better.

It was early Saturday evening. The line of gray cloud had lifted, revealing a band of blue sky along the horizon. The sea spread towards that line like a swath of ruffled satin. The air smelled deliciously fresh. I could hear the bang and clang of men preparing their boats for the dawn run. Lori and her dad were there, too. I saw them moving about on the deck of the Lori-Girl, heard their laughter.

Geoff's ragout would be a while. I decided to follow Sheba to the wharf and thank Lori again for driving me to the vet's to pick up my cat.

I quickly changed out of my funeral clothes and ran across to the wharf.

"Hey, Gailynn, you come to accuse anybody else of murdering Doc?" shouted Tom Gunn, the owner of the Cindy-Lou.

"Yeah, I was getting my hernia fixed in Halifax that week," Tom's brother, Keith, hollered. "Maybe it was me."

They laughed, as did everyone else within hearing distance. I stiffened my spine and called to Lori, "Hey."

"Hey yourself," she said. Taking the final bite out of her apple, she tossed the core. "Coming aboard?"

She knew very well the answer was no. "Just wanted to say thanks again for taking me to fetch Sheba."

"How's she doing?"

I waved my hand towards the trucks. "Out hunting again."

"Glad to hear it. Don't you let those guys get to you, Gai. You keep hunting, too. Between you and Andrew, I'm sure Doc's killer will get his due. Look, Dad and I've got to get this stuff done before it's dark, though, Gailynn. Mind?"

"No, of course not." I left my friend and her non-father stacking boxes of something on the lobster boat's cramped deck and I wandered along the wharf, killing time. I was glad no one else spoke to me. I'd endured quite enough embarrassment for one day. I reached the end, turned and started back when I spotted Bud disembarking. He hesitated before striding towards me. From the set of his shoulders, I knew he had a message to deliver.

I braced myself.

"Look, Gailynn, I like you and all, you're my daughter's best friend, but I gotta tell you she's givin' you bad advice. Steer clear of Doc's murder or you're gonna live to regret it."

I felt my eyes go wide. "Are you threatening me?"

"I'm tellin' you the truth. Girl, someone's already done poisoned your cat and trashed your fancy glass shop. How much more's it gonna take to get the message through that thick head of yours?" He shook his head regretfully. "Lori's got her mama's beauty and brains, thank heavens, but you, girl, you make the gulls look like geniuses."

"Gee, thanks, Bud."

"It's the truth, girl. And the more you keep stickin' your nose where it don't belong, the more everyone's gonna know it, too."

"I'm sorry but I can't stand by and do nothing while Doc's killer gets off scott free."

"Well, maybe he's not scott free. Maybe he's feelin' guilty and scared. You keep up and he's gonna feel cornered, too. And if'n he's guilty and scared and cornered he's likely to do anything to keep his secret secret."

"And that makes it OK?"

"No it don't make it OK, it just makes it understandable. We all got secrets, girl, even you and me. None of us wants people stickin' their noses in. That's why we call 'em secrets."

I dug my fists into my pockets. "I don't have any secrets."

"Well I do and I sure as the blazes don't want you findin' out."

"I already know." It just popped out. I slapped my hand over my mouth but it was too late, Bud had heard.

He leaned close and his liquored breath set my

teeth on edge. "You know what, girl?"

"Nothing," I said.

"Girl, you're a terrible liar. You know that?"

I stared at my shuffling feet, wishing I could escape the inevitable. I'd come to the wharf to convince myself Geoff's theory of Lori's parentage was completely bogus. If I just watched Lori and her dad I'd see all these familial similarities that would prove Bud was Lori's biological father. I'd observe silently. Maybe ask a subtle question or two, but that was all. I was not going to confront Lori or her dad with Geoff's theory. And I certainly wasn't going to accuse anyone of anything. I was not going to make a scene twice in one day.

But my brain short-circuited and there they were, the things I didn't want to say, pouring out my mouth. Was I really as dumb as a herring gull?

Apparently so.

"I—I learn things at the clinic," I said quietly. "But I would never tell anyone. Honest. Especially not Lori."

Bud's eyes narrowed to slits.

I leaned closer despite his atrociously foul breath. This was between Bud and me. No one else would hear. "I promise I will *never* tell Lori."

Bud's face went white, then red then purple, as though he was about to explode. He grabbed me by the neck, saying words only fishermen knew, and shook.

I thought I was dead.

But as suddenly as he grabbed me, his fingers opened and he shoved me away.

I stumbled backwards, arms flailing, and flew over the wharf's raised cement edge.

31

The water slammed my ears. It rushed up my nose. It surged through my clothes. It closed over my head, sucking me downwards into its oily, icy abyss. My hair slithered around my face like Medusa's snakes. My sodden shoes dragged me deeper. My bursting lungs screamed for release. I closed my eyes as the blackness swallowed me whole.

I heard another explosion. Hands grabbed me. Arms held me. Legs kicked, moving me up, up, up until I broke the surface and blessed, frigid air filled my face. Gasping, sobbing, I sucked it in.

"Breathe, Gailynn, breathe." Lori bobbed in the water with me. One arm firmly around my ribs, she wiped my hair from my eyes. "You're OK, Gai. I have you."

I threw my arms around her neck and almost drowned us again.

Lori wriggled free, grabbed the back of my jacket and gave me a sharp jerk. "I have you, Gai, but you have to let me tow you to the boat. OK?"

She slid her arm around my neck, keeping my chin out of the water, and I gripped that arm with all my might.

"OK, OK."

Lori towed me to the Lori-Girl. A rope ladder bumped against the boat's side and she hiked me out of the water enough to grab it. I pulled myself up, tumbled over the boat's gunwale onto its deck and lay on my side, curled into a fetal position. Breathing was all I could manage.

Things on the deck seemed oddly distorted, as though I saw them through a wobbly telescope and I tried making sense of boxes, paint cans, apple cores, an empty bottle of Arran Island Malt Whiskey and coiled rope.

"Here, Gai, sit up and let's get you out of that wet coat."

Lori, also soaked, dragged me into a sitting position and tried peeling my jacket from me. It didn't come off. I guess the seawater had glued my clothes together and she couldn't remove the outer layer without the shirt and sweater underneath.

We were both shivering, our teeth rattling noisily.

"Stand up," she ordered. "I can't do this unless you stand up."

So I did. Shaking, totally discombobulated, I staggered to my feet on the boat's shifting deck. As it lurched and I stumbled, reality hit me like another slam into icy water.

I was on a boat.

Lori recognized my terror a split second after I did. She tried to catch me before I threw myself back into the ocean in my panic to get off the boat, but I batted her hands away.

"Let me go." I heard my voice rising. "Let me go!"

She stepped back in surrender.

I scrambled over the Lori-Girl's side, my numb fingers clinging to the sanded wood rail. Keith and Tom Gunn reached for me, dropping me onto my feet on the wharf. I could have kissed the scarred cement. I could have kissed Keith and Tom until I realized the two were laughing at me.

"Kinda early in the year for swimmin', ain't it Gailynn?"

I unclamped my fingers from each man's shirtsleeves. With the greatest effort I had ever exerted for any cause, I lifted my chin. "I thought it was time."

They hugged their bellies and chortled like idiots. You'd think I'd just said the funniest thing in the universe.

"What's so funny?" asked Sam, drawn to the sound of their laughter.

"Gailynn, here," said Tom. "She's finally gone decided she's gonna take up swimmin'."

Teeth chattering, face burning, I squared my shoulders and marched away, but the squish-squish of each step only made them laugh harder.

Lori ran to catch up with me and we met Geoff hustling down his back stairs, blankets in hand.

"I saw," was all he said as he handed Lori one blanket and wrapped the second around me.

I folded into his welcome arms, pressing my face against his chest. I felt his cheek against my wet hair and his breath, oh so warm against my scalp. I tied to act brave, but I don't think my hiccoughing breaths fooled him.

"Dad threw her into the water. I don't know what's got into him." Lori's chattering teeth punctuated each word. "He's so unpredictable these days he scares me."

"We need to get the two of you inside and out of those wet clothes. Gailynn, where's your key?" Geoff drew me back far enough to ask.

My fingers couldn't manage my zippered pocket

so he opened it for me.

He let us in the back door of Dunmaglass. "Take her upstairs and get yourselves warm. I'll be right back."

With a kiss to my nose he left us to fend for ourselves. I didn't know what he was off to do and frankly, at that moment, I didn't care.

Lori half pushed me up the stairs to my apartment. She set the shower on full and shoved me in, clothes and all.

"Don't come out until you stop shivering," she ordered. "There will be dry clothes waiting."

"What about you?" I asked from behind the shower's sliding glass door.

"I'll borrow some sweats and change in your bedroom. I'm not as cold as you. I'll be fine."

Then Lori left me too, and I was alone with the hot water and steam, and fear.

Phobias are an odd thing. No matter how logical or matter-of-fact you pretend to be they sneak up on you and before you realize it, you're in full panic mode. There's no escape, no way around, you have to pass though them. Something I'd learned as a kid wriggled its way through my memory. A Bible verse my old Sunday school teacher made me memorize, what was it?

When you pass through the waters I shall be with you and through the rivers they won't overtake you.

I repeated it out loud, surprisingly calmed by the promise, now that I was safe in my shower. If only I'd had the presence of mind to remember it while I was drowning.

I'd been so sure I was going to die.

When I was a kid, I went out on the boat with Dad

and Sam. I wasn't paying attention. I wasn't doing what I was told, and somehow my foot got tangled in the cable that winds through the edge of the net. Don't ask me how. To this day Dad still can't figure it out. But when the weighted net went over the edge into the ocean, I went with it.

Dad dove in and cut me free but by the time he got me back into the boat, I was basically dead. Sam says Dad did mouth-to-mouth on me for half an hour before I started breathing on my own again. Sam says he's never seen Dad that scared before or since. But me, I get that scared every time I think of climbing aboard a boat. Every time I see one bob on the water, I feel that rope tighten around my ankles and my feet yank out from under me. Every time I think of even wading into the sea I feel the weight of the waves over my head and the tug of the nets dragging me to the bottom.

Would I ever stop shivering?

Layer by layer, the hot water penetrated deeper. I slowly peeled off my clothes. I soaped and lathered and scrubbed away every trace of sea. The grunge from my hair, the stench from my skin, the chill from my bones. I even brushed my teeth in the shower. Finally my tremors stopped.

Had I really passed through the waters? I wiped the fog from the mirror and stared at my reflection. I was alive. I sat on the edge of the tub, unable to find words enough to thank God for sending Lori to save me.

True to her promise she'd left a neat pile of dry duds for me on the bathroom counter. I toweled off, pulled on the fuzzy jammies and housecoat, and blow-dried my hair. When I came out of the bathroom, I found Geoff and Lori sitting in my living room drinking tea. Her right hand was freshly bandaged, she wore my faded navy sweats, but otherwise she looked no worse for the icy swim.

Geoff jumped to his feet immediately. He felt my forehead, smoothed my hair over my shoulders. "Woman, I've never been so scared in my entire life." He hugged me tight and it felt so good I could have stayed in his arms forever. But he pushed me away. "I want you to take these tablets, drink this tea and tuck yourself into bed for the night. Understand?"

"I'm OK. Really."

Neither he, nor Lori for that matter, looked convinced.

"There are two doctors giving you this order, Gailynn," he said. "And Lori's going to spend the night on your couch to make sure you obey."

I sighed and swallowed Geoff's tablets with sips of sickly sweet tea. "What did you put in this?"

"Sugar. You were shivering so badly I was afraid you were going into shock." He kept stroking my hair.

"Well, I'm OK, now," I told him again. "You and Lori don't have to mother me."

"I told you she'd be ornery," Lori said.

"Lori stays," Geoff said to me.

The mug in my hand wasn't too steady and tea slopped over the rim onto the floor.

"See?" He took it from me. "Now, to bed with you. Lori will lock the door behind me and then come and say goodnight. By then you should be tucked into bed with the covers up to your chin. Understand?"

I didn't argue, which meant he was right. I did need to rest. "I'm sorry about supper," I said.

Deep lines bracketed his mouth. "Just promise me you'll be here to do it tomorrow." He cupped my cheeks with his hands.

Too muddled to decipher his mood, I closed my eyes. The warmth of his palms against my skin comforted me. "I promise."

That's the last I remember until the inevitable nightmare woke me up. I found Sheba asleep on my chest. No doubt her bulk against my ribs triggered the dream. I stroked her silky fur, drawing reassurance. I was alive. As I drifted back to sleep I heard Lori moving about in the other room.

****

Saturday's fiasco left me frightened and bewildered. My best friend's father had tried to kill me. Setting aside his grief over his wife's passing, and his penchant for overindulging, I was inclined to think his reaction still somewhat extreme since all I'd done was imply I knew he wasn't Lori's biological father. In fact, come to think of it, if I remembered correctly I hadn't even said that much. I'd simply whispered I knew his secret. In a shamefully tactless way that breached every ethical boundary Geoff had tried to drum into my thick head, I'll admit, but certainly no bald-faced declaration. My comment was inappropriate, rude, obnoxious, highly improper, but worth killing over? I thought not.

Yet that's what Bud had tried to do—strangle and drown me.

Lori had headed home once she was sure I'd survived the night. I was disappointed I'd missed Geoff singing at church, but glad in a way. I didn't think I could face people after yesterday.

Wow, was it really only yesterday I accused Mimi

of murdering Doc?

I let Sheba out, pulled on my freshly washed jacket over my sweater and jeans—I guess Lori did my laundry while I slept—and went for a walk alone. I did not go to the beach. Instead, I strode straight up McCormick Street to Murray, and out of town towards the cemetery. In the midst of yesterday's drama I'd missed saying good-bye to Doc. I thought now would be a fine time to do so.

My grief felt heavier than ever. It pressed down on me, like the horrible weight of the sea closing over my head.

I prayed as I walked. And as I prayed, I realized the burden I felt was shame, not grief. Shame for the way I was treating the people I loved. I'd been spying on them, calculating their every word and action as a motive for murder. What right did I have to judge my neighbors? Was that why Geoff had looked so weary last night?

He saw. That's what he'd said when he rushed down with the blanket. He saw me talking to Bud. No doubt he believed he saw me breach the clinic's patient confidentiality rule, breaking my promise that I could be trusted. It would be useless to try to convince him I hadn't actually told Bud anything. Bud's reaction contradicted any denial I could make.

And in all honesty, I couldn't claim innocence. I had bent Geoff's rule. It was Bud's hands on my neck that kept me from smashing it completely.

Lord, forgive me.

The burden eased a little.

It was wrong to say anything to Bud. Whatever happened between Doc Campbell and Ellen Fisher all those years ago had no bearing on what was going on now. I needed to get a grip on myself. I needed to leave the past to the past.

Lori's parentage had nothing to do with Doc's murder so I would just forget the whole sordid thing.

My steps slowed as I neared the cemetery. Then why did Bud Fisher want me dead?

Only one reason presented itself. Bud found out about Ellen and Doc's affair and murdered Doc in a jealous drunken rage.

Except, why now? If Doc and Ellen had their fling twenty-five years ago, why get upset now? Ellen made a deathbed confession? Was that how Bud found out about Lori? Or maybe Doc and Ellen's affair never actually ended. Bud put it together at Ellen's funeral. I'd told Geoff there was no way Lori's mom had fooled around on her husband but really, what did I know? Maybe I'd grown so accustomed to her adultery I never saw a thing.

I mulled over the possibility. On the one hand was Bud's increased drinking since Ellen's death. On the other hand...what? Lori was living breathing proof Ellen Fisher fooled around on her husband, but if no one suspected her why would Ellen confess? Scratch that. Reverend Innes always says guilt weighs especially heavy when you're dying. I tried to picture Ellen and Doc at the clinic, the way they related, the way they looked at each other, the way they both looked at Lori.

Did Doc look at Lori like an adoring father? Like Bud did?

Maybe Doc didn't know about Lori anymore than Bud knew about Doc. I shook my head. I was making things up.

I stopped beside Doc's grave. Fake green carpet

covered the mounded dirt. Several wreaths and bouquets rested where the tombstone would eventually stand.

"Did you know, Doc?"

Naturally, he didn't answer.

If Bud Fisher discovered his wife had been unfaithful and if he realized the daughter he adored was not his own, and if he learned the man who'd cuckolded him was the same man who backed out of Hum Harbour Holes, causing him to lose all the money he'd invested so he could buy his beloved daughter a medical practice, could Bud become angry enough to retaliate? I felt Bud's hands around my neck.

The problem was Doc's murder was not a momentary act of fury. It was premeditated.

When Bud grabbed me, his anger flamed then died. I'd seen it wash from his eyes the instant before he pushed me away. The part where I almost drowned was more my doing than Bud's. If I'd kept my footing or kept my head, I would have managed just fine. It was my personal phobia that turned the dunking into a nightmare.

But just because that one time Bud's anger cooled as fast as it blazed, didn't mean he was incapable of the slow burning kind, given the right circumstances. Like when he was drunk. I wrapped my arms around my waist trying to rekindle the warmth I felt when Geoff was near. I was very thankful Geoff did not imbibe.

I found myself staring at the stone bench where Geoff and I'd sat and talked and I remembered Bud Fisher driving along the cemetery's back access road. I'd assumed he was visiting Ellen's grave and thought no more of the event. But now I remembered Bud throwing something out of his truck window as he drove along.

I left Doc and went searching.

It took a while, but I finally found an empty whiskey bottle in the tall grass at the edge of the cemetery. It was an empty bottle of Canadian Club and it got me thinking.

31

Andrew's crime scene people had taken lots of photos of Doc's boat before they collected and catalogued everything in sight and I assumed Andrew had those photos or at least a list of what had been found. I wanted to see that list.

Like Bud Fisher, Doc was a finicky drinker. Bud drank Canadian Club and Doc drank Arran Island Scotch Whiskey, a single malt he had the local liquor store stock especially for him. I knew this because Doc sometimes had me pick up his bottle when he was running behind schedule. I wasn't sure how many others knew of Doc's preference.

It was about a mile from the cemetery to the cop shop and I hoofed it purposefully. With each step, I grew more certain that Doc's liquor was the clue that would lead us to his murderer. Hadn't Andrew said the poison was wood alcohol? What better way to administer poison than hide it in Doc's liquor.

A cloud bank was collecting in the eastern sky but the May sun still shone brightly overhead. I unbuttoned my jacket, letting the wind cool my neck and lift my hair. Sundays are a quiet day in Hum Harbour. We're a traditional community, where people set aside their work for the Sabbath. Despite recent Sunday shopping laws, most stores are closed and the Hubris Heron only serves a light brunch to the après-church crowd.

The cop shop's also on weekend detail. Rose McKenna has her weekends off and Kenny Stewart, a local college student, fills in as dispatcher. Kenny wants to be a cop like Andrew and he's a little hyper about protocol. I wasn't sure whether Andrew would be in his office and I knew Kenny would refuse me entry if he wasn't. Kenny Stewart is a formidable challenge.

I fluffed my hair and moistened my lips before pushing open the police station door. "Hey, Kenny, how's it going?"

"Ms. MacDonald, hello."

Kenny called everyone by their formal name when he worked. Any other time he'd have said, "Hey, Gai."

"Andrew in?"

Kenny checked the log. He could have just turned his head and looked.

"Not at the moment. He shouldn't be long."

"Oh yeah? I'll wait in his office, then." I rounded the counter but Kenny zoomed into position, barring my way.

"Sorry, Ms. MacDonald, but I can't allow you to wait in Officer MacDonald's office. You understand."

"Relax, Kenny. Andrew won't mind." I tried stepping around his bulky frame.

"Sorry, ma'am, but I have orders. No one is allowed in the offices unsupervised."

"Who would give you a silly order like that?"

"Your brother, after the last time I let you wait in there by yourself. I got in big trouble."

I tried to look innocent. "How long am I going to have to stand around, then?"

"I can bring you a chair." Kenny scooted into the

back office to drag one out. I followed and almost got bowled over for my effort. "Sorry," he said again.

Nothing left for it, I obediently sat and waited. I crossed my legs. I examined my cuticles. I tapped my toe. I memorized the Ten Steps to a Safe Apprehension poster on the wall. I watched the hands on the clock slooowly tick away the hour.

Kenny kept himself busy at the computer.

"What are you doing that's so important?" I finally asked.

"Filing these reports." He indicated a stack of paperwork beside him.

"You're allowed to do that? I thought they'd be confidential."

He kept his eyes on the monitor's screen. "Since I started my second semester criminology course Officer MacDonald lets me do these for him."

"Does he really?" I sauntered over. "I guess parking tickets aren't so confidential Andrew need worry."

"Parking tickets? No way. This stuff is bigger than that." He nervously glanced both ways and I leaned closer. "I'm transcribing his reports from the murder investigation onto official RCMP triple copy forms."

"Triple copy forms, eh? Wow."

"Yeah, cool, eh?"

I agreed enthusiastically. "Are they very different from our usual form?" I said *our* in the hope he'd let down his guard. *Our* forms, *our* officers, *our* side, established me as one of the in crowd.

"Not very. See here?" Kenny pointed out numerous similarities between our three-copy report and theirs. What interested me more, however, was what Andrew and Kenny recorded on those three copy reports.

According to the detailed list of items confiscated from the Medical Convention there was one empty liquor bottle. In his report, Andrew noted this, drawing the inference that one bottle of Canadian Club would not be enough liquor to incapacitate a seasoned alcoholic like Douglas Campbell. He did not however, comment on the significance of the brand of whiskey found on Doc's boat.

That meant I knew two things my brother didn't. I was about to help myself to a note pad and leave him a message when Andrew strolled into the cop shop.

"What do you think you're doing?" he bellowed so loud Kenny knocked the delete button when he jumped. The computer screen emptied.

Kenny snapped to attention and his chair tumbled backwards. "Officer MacDonald, sir. Your sister is awaiting you, sir."

I thought he might salute.

"What did I tell you about keeping her out of this part of the office? What is there about O-U-T that you don't understand, Mr. Stewart?"

Poor Kenny stammered and stuttered, unable to enunciate even the simplest excuse for my presence behind the counter, or the fact that I was peering over his shoulder reading police documents. And as I watched my five foot eight inch brother humiliate six foot three inch Kenny Stewart I decided anyone as pushy and arrogant as Andrew did not deserve help solving Doc's murder. He'd have to find another way to impress the RCMP.

So, armed with the information I desired, I exited the Hum Harbour Police Station while my brother continued haranguing poor Kenny Stewart.

I no longer felt guilty for reading Andrew's official three copy reports. I would take the information I'd gleaned and my superior awareness of Doctor Douglas Campbell's drinking habits with me. I would confront my fear and intentionally board the Lori-Girl. Yes, I would go back to the Lori-Girl and collect the empty bottle of Arran Island Scotch Whiskey lying on the deck. It could only have gotten there if Bud traded liquor bottles with Doc, taking the tainted Arran Island bottle back to the Lori-Girl with him and leaving his own harmless Canadian Club in its place. And I would wave Doc's empty Arran Island Scotch Whiskey bottle under Andrew's nose. I would prove once and for all that I was as capable as anyone else of doing something right.

I would stop at the clinic and grab a bag and some sterile gloves. I didn't want Andrew accusing me of compromising the evidence by getting my fingerprints on the bottle. And, come to think of it, I would bring Geoff along as an eyewitness, in case there were any questions.

Pleased, no, *thrilled* with my plan I buttoned my coat tight and marched down the hill. The cold wind from the east was picking up.

****

I found Geoff at the clinic. He sat behind his paper-strewn desk studying a legal-looking document. He came around the desk and kissed me hello. I quite liked that.

"Glad to see you looking yourself again. How'd you sleep?"

"I don't know what you gave me but I slept

through 'til after lunch. I'm sorry I missed hearing you at church."

"Don't worry about it." Then he frowned. "There's a gleam in your eye, Gailynn. What are you up to?"

I told him about the liquor bottle I'd seen on the Lori-Girl. How Bud Fisher had poisoned Doc's Arran Island Scotch Whiskey.

"Bud removed the contaminated bottle and replaced it with one of his own empties. No one suspected a thing. There was the empty liquor bottle rolling around the deck of the Medical Convention, which we all assumed was Doc's. It wasn't until I saw the empty Arran Island bottle lying on the Lori-Girl that I put it together."

"And you're absolutely sure Doc drank only Arran Island Scotch?"

"He called everything else cow swill. He would have dumped Bud's Canadian Club into the ocean without tasting it."

"Who, besides you, would know about Doc's preference?"

"The liquor store, Ellen Fisher. And she could easily have told Bud."

Geoff nodded. "It makes sense." He shuffled some papers and passed me one. "Read this."

I'm not used to legalese so I read it carefully. It was a signed affidavit stating Lori Fisher was Doctor Douglas James Campbell's daughter. It called Lori the biological product of a three-year affair between Ellen Fisher and Doc. The affidavit was dated the week before Ellen Fisher died.

"There's our motive," I said. "Bud found out about Doc and Ellen and he killed Doc out of jealousy."

"That's not all I found." Geoff handed me another

document. "In this one Doc agrees to assume financial responsibility for Lori should Ellen and or Bud die before Lori is established in her desired career."

I sank into the chair opposite Geoff and read that two-page document.

"What exactly does this mean?"

"It means Ellen got Doc to commit to Lori's future. I don't know if he knew about Lori's parentage before Ellen's death-bed affidavit, but it indicates Doc knew all about Lori when he sold me the practice."

"Doesn't selling to you go against everything he promised Ellen?"

"That's what I thought, too, until I found this."

I glanced vaguely at the next stack of papers he handed me. "Where did you find all of these?"

"I got these copies from Marjorie Campbell after church. Apparently she's executor of Doc's will and his lawyer passed all Doc's documentation onto her after yesterday's funeral."

"And she gave them to you?"

"We had lunch together and talked and she told me all about Doc and Ellen and Lori's trust fund."

"Trust fund?"

"Yes, Doc established a trust fund in Lori's name. Apparently, he wanted a few stipulations on how she could spend the money, which would not be possible with a straight inheritance. He was determined to keep the money out of Bud's hands."

I scanned the first page. "Is that what all this is?"

"Flip to the end."

I did.

It was a bill of sale deeding partnership shares in a fully established medical practice in Halifax to Doctor Lori Ann Fisher. Paid in full.

I gasped when I saw the price tag. "That was why Doc pulled out of Hum Harbour Holes and left town! Once Ellen died he was committed to guaranteeing Lori's future and he couldn't keep that commitment if he lost everything in his malpractice suit with Sam and Sasha."

Geoff nodded.

"I've gotta tell Lori."

"Gailynn, maybe you should leave it to the lawyers. They should be the ones to tell her about Doc's will."

"You think that would be easier for her?"

"I think it's their job, not yours."

"But telling her about Doc and the trust fund and the practice in Halifax, I think that would come better from me."

"Maybe."

"Knowing won't help when Andrew arrests her father, but it's the least I can do."

"All right," he said, although with obvious reluctance. "You go to Lori and I'll take what we know, these papers and your information about Doc's whiskey, to Andrew. If you're with her when she finds out that Andrew's arrested Bud, she won't have to face that alone."

I held out my hand. "Agreed."

Geoff clasped my outstretched hand and his gaze held mine. "Have you solved the second mystery yet?"

The most delicious shiver slid up my spine. It had nothing to do with Doc or Lori and everything to do with the electricity zapping through the air between us. I'd never felt anything so intense in my entire life and a corner of my brain wondered if I was suffering a post traumatic reaction after yesterday's near death experience.

"I think so," I said.

Geoff pulled me into his arms.

By the time I left Geoff collecting the papers to take to Andrew, I was floating six feet off the ground.

32

Ominous clouds boiled overhead and wind battered the flags that lined Main Street. My hair whipped out behind me like one of them. Coming straight out of the east the wind brought tears to my eyes and I turned up my collar around my ears, shrinking into my coat. I could see white caps churning the cove and the fishing boats bucking against the wharf. I recognized the Lori-Girl as the only boat with a light burning so I headed there.

Gulls love rough weather. They ride the wind and dive at the waves. Some even bob on the water like comical little paddleboats. When it's really rough, though, they head inland. As I strolled down the wharf, my hands deep in my pockets, I noted that's exactly what the gulls were up to, fleeing for cover.

It wasn't yet seven, and the eastern sky was indigo. A good night for staying safe inside my apartment making earring molds, I decided. Thanks to Doc's murder and my involvement in Andrew's investigation, I'd ignored my craft this last week. Time to get back on track. Maybe Lori would like to spend the night again. She was great help sorting through my collection. She had an amazing eye for color variations.

I stopped beside the Lori-Girl. Despite the light glowing inside the cabin, I couldn't see my friend.

"Hey, Lori," I called.

The sea smelled angry. Foaming waves bashed the boats against the wood pylons.

I cupped my hands and shouted louder. "Lori, it's me. You can't believe what I just found out."

I saw movement at the corner of my eye and I spun around in surprise. Lori was standing beside me, her dad's red metal toolbox in her hand.

"Dad's passed out. I have to tie all this stuff down myself before this storm hits." She looked, well, relieved, which I thought odd, considering.

I swallowed, reaching deep for courage. "Let me help."

The way the wind twisted her laugh it sounded cruel. "You? Don't be stupid, Gailynn. You can't help me."

"Sure I can," I said, silently begging God to carry me through this. But while I prayed another section of my brain was busy wondering how much help Lori'd let me be if she knew Andrew was right now, arresting her dad for Doc's murder. Would she ever trust me again? Her attitude towards Geoff proved she could harbor a grudge for an awfully long time.

"I came to tell you what Geoff and I have found out. Doc bought you a medical practice in Halifax!"

She pushed her hair out of her eyes. "Yes, I know.

"You do? Then why are you so mad about Geoff? I mean, a practice in Halifax or Hum Harbour—is there a choice here?"

"Doc promised me the Harbour practice and Geoff convinced him to break his word."

"No he didn't."

"Then why did Doc tell me Geoff had?"

"I don't know. Maybe he lied because he sensed you'd be disappointed."

"Right." Her toneless laugh left me uncertain.

"It's true. Geoff found all the paperwork. Doc even left you a trust fund. Can you believe it?"

"I've got work to do." She turned away from me.

I nabbed her wrist. "Didn't you hear me? Doc's bought you a practice in Halifax and set you up with a trust fund. No more boat scraping. No more worrying about your student loans."

The wind lashed her hair into a tangle. "He thought he could buy me off, but it was too little, too late. That's what I told him."

"You think Doc did all that to buy you off?" I asked, completely missing the significance of what she'd said. "For what?"

"He said he'd only just found out about me. Mom's deathbed confession. What did he think I was? Stupid? Look at me! Everyday I see this face in the mirror. Everyday I see *his* chin under *my* nose. He knew whose kid I was. From the moment I was born, he knew."

I stared at her lovely dimpled chin.

"I told him if he wouldn't acknowledge me then, he wasn't going to start messing my life up now." She shifted the toolbox to her right hand and it swung back and forth like a pendulum.

"Mess up your life? He was trying to help you."

"Like you're going to help me?"

"Yes," I said. "Doc obviously made a promise to your mom and he was going to keep it."

"Baloney. He was appeasing his conscience."

The tarp covering the boxes on the Lori-Girl's deck tore free and Lori swore. I released her wrist in surprise.

"Look at that. Now my stuff's going to get all

wet." She tried elbowing past me but I grabbed her arm this time.

"Those are your moving boxes. What are you doing?"

"For once in your life, Gailynn, mind your own business."

The gale howled in our ears. It whipped the blue plastic tarp to bits. Suddenly details began falling bang, bang, bang into place.

"Lori, when did you find out about Doc's trust fund?"

"What difference does it make?"

"When did you talk to him?"

She shook my hand away. "Get off my back, Gailynn."

"It's important. If you were the last person to see Doc, Andrew needs to know."

"Why? So he can screw up my life, too?"

"Lori, he's about to arrest your dad for Doc's murder. If we go back now, you can still save him."

Lori swung the toolbox.

33

The next thing I noticed was the frighteningly familiar smell of diesel fuel and turpentine. It burned my nose. Then the unforgettable lurch you only experience on a boat. I jerked fully awake. My head felt like a cracked coconut, or at least what I imagined a cracked coconut felt like. Rolling onto my side I threw up.

This couldn't be real.

But it was. I opened my eyes and there I lay on the deck of the Lori-Girl. I could see my friend standing in the boat's cabin, hands on the wheel, legs akimbo. She must have been hanging on tight because every time the boat climbed and tumbled over another wave she barely swayed.

Me, I slid around the deck with the toolbox. When I slammed against Lori's packing crates, I managed to rise to my knees and crawl towards her.

"Lori, take me home."

She kept her back to me as though she didn't know I was there. The old lobster boat groaned as it crashed into the next wave and I hit the cabin's doorframe full force to my ribs. Lori must have heard me holler because she turned.

"Come in," she invited.

I slowly got to my feet, still gripping the doorframe.

"We have to go back."

She shifted the throttle. The Lori-Girl's engine droned louder.

Gripping the walls, I worked my way around the tiny cabin until I stood beside her.

"Lori, we have to go back and tell Andrew what you know. He's arresting your dad."

I thought I saw her hesitate but I could have been wrong, it passed so quickly. The boat lurched and I fell against her.

Lori shoved me away so hard I bounced off the wall.

"What's wrong with you?"

She glared at me in apparent amazement. "You, your runt of a brother, and everyone else in Hum Harbour. How's that for starters?"

I raked my hair out of my eyes. Lori's golden waves encircled her head in a tangled web. Her face glowed an eerie green in the reflected light from the boat's dials. She looked alien. The snarling twist of her lips and the cold edge in her voice sounded alien, too.

"You betrayed me, Gailynn, just like everyone else. I thought you were different, but you're not."

"I betrayed you?"

"You think Doc's stupid practice in Halifax makes up for what you've done with Geoff Grant?"

"What did I do?"

"You stole my dream. You stole Hum Harbour from me."

I touched her arm, but she glared at my hand as though it were the hand of the devil. Claws out, she drew blood when she yanked me away.

I jerked free and pressed my wounded hand against my lips. Now I wasn't just afraid of the sea and the boat, I was afraid of Lori, too.

"We have to go back, Lori. We have to help your dad."

"Nothing's going to happen to my father. Any theories you and your ridiculous brother have concocted are rubbish. They'll never hold up in court."

"What are you talking about?"

She gave me her coldest look, the one she saves for imbeciles and fools. "OK, tell me what you think you know."

I went back to gripping the doorframe. "Your dad tampered with Doc's whiskey. Then, after Doc drank the poisoned liquor, your dad replaced the doctored bottle with an empty of his own. Andrew found that bottle on the Medical Convention."

"So."

"And I saw Doc's poisoned empty is here on the Lori-Girl."

"When?"

"When you dragged me aboard the Lori-Girl after you rescued me."

"There is no way you can prove which bottle is which," she said as she adjusted our heading.

"Sure I can. Just like your dad only drinks CC, Doc never touched anything except Arran Island Malt. Ever."

She shifted the throttle. "That still doesn't prove anything."

"It will when Andrew takes possession of the empty Arran Malt off the Lori-Girl. I bet they'll even be able to find traces of the methyl alcohol inside it."

Lori's brows puckered into an angry V. "Then where's Doc's empty?"

Releasing the doorframe with one hand, I pointed.

"Back there."

Lori barely took a moment to digest what I said before she grabbed a length of rope tied to a metal ring on the wall. After looping the cord over one of the steering wheel's spokes, she marched to the back of the boat.

I watched her rifle around, kicking aside a pile of rope, poking the ruined tarp. She came up with a case marked Canadian Club. From that she pulled Doc's empty bottle of Arran Island Malt. Apparently her dad had stashed it with his other bottles.

"I'd planned to ditch this once I got farther out," she shouted. Sliding the bottle back into the crate, she shoved the box towards the rail.

I knew Lori loved her dad more than anything, but if she pitched those bottles into the water she'd be destroying evidence. Who knew what would happen to her.

The Lori-Girl chugged past the breakwater. As Lori braced her feet so she wouldn't be bumped off balance, I threw myself across the deck. I banged into her awkwardly, knocking her to her knees. The box hit the deck and skidded out of reach.

At that same instant, the sky opened. Cold, hard rain drenched us in an instant. The Lori-Girl pitched this way and that on the churning water. Half the north Atlantic sloshed over the gunwales.

"What do you think you're doing?" she shouted, her teeth chattering.

"Trying to save you from jail." I yelled back over the Lori-Girl's straining engine.

"I can look after myself." She edged towards the box of bottles. "Once I dump this evidence there'll be no proof anyone did anything."

"But there's still me. I'll have to tell Andrew what I know."

Wind driven rain pelted us in sheets. Frigid water swirled across the Lori-Girl's deck. The boat's running lights barely pricked the darkness, yet as Lori turned, I saw pure hatred in her face.

Water crashed over my head, blinding me. When the wave receded and I shoved my hair out of my eyes, I saw Lori towering over me.

She surveyed me in mock dismay. "Poor Gailynn, nothing ever works the way you hope." Another wave slammed the boat. The chilling blast distracted her long enough for me to scrunch myself into the narrow slot between Lori's moving boxes and the stern. I thought I'd be safe there.

But like she said, nothing ever works out quite the way you hope...

Instead of saving myself I'd tangled myself in a pile of rope. The harder I tried to wrench free, the tauter it coiled around my legs. Tighter and tighter with every jerk. It was my worst nightmare.

Lori stepped towards me. I kept my attention glued to her face while my hands groped for anything that might help me.

"You can't win, Gai, you know that. I always come out on top."

My fingers closed around something long and sturdy. It felt like a pole, maybe the gaff. I shifted position and Lori thought I was shrinking from her.

"Can't get away anymore, Gailynn. I have you cornered."

"No," I said.

"We're going to get this over with nice and fast." She gripped the front of my jacket and hoisted me to my feet.

"No." I squirmed, wriggled, bucked.

"Cut it out or you're going to hurt both of us," she snapped.

She didn't see the pole in my hands. As she wrapped her arms around my waist and lifted me, the gaff jammed into one of her boxes and stuck.

Lori's feet skidded sideways on the water-soaked deck and she stumbled backwards, whacking her head against the gunwale. The crack rang so loud it echoed over the screaming wind, waves and boat engine. Then she slithered limply to the deck.

God, don't let her be dead.

I crawled to her, dragging the rope with me. I felt her throat and found a thundering pulse.

Wiping tears of relief from my eyes, I unraveled enough line and tied Lori to me and me to the boat, leaving enough rope between us to do what I must. Then I crawled to the cabin.

I don't know boats. The dials, switches and levers might as well be from a space ship. But, by trial and error, I found the radio and called "Mayday."

Then I turned the Lori-Girl around and chugged her back to the tiny spark of light in the distance I knew to be Hum Harbour.

34

The police car's flashing blue lights guided me in. Andrew, Sasha, Sam and Geoff stood on the wharf.

Sam shouted for me to cut the Lori-Girl's engines and let her drift. I did as I was told. As the lobster boat banged hard against the pylons, he jumped aboard and tied her to the wharf.

Andrew jumped onboard and crouched beside Lori, who lay where I'd left her. As best as I could tell, she hadn't moved since I tied her up. Andrew waved Geoff aboard and the two conferred about taking her to the hospital. Waiting for the ambulance would mean a half hour delay, minimum. Could they afford to wait?

"Does she need a back board?" Andrew asked. "We have one at the station. I could get Rose and the boys to bring it down. Lori'd have to go to Antigonish in the hearse but—"

At the mention of the hearse, Lori's eyes fluttered open. She pushed the men away and sat up. Maybe she hadn't been unconscious after all.

"I do not need a stretcher or a hearse." She poked Andrew. "Untie my legs."

He began obediently picking at the mass of knots. "Gai, did you do this?"

"She'd hit her head and I was afraid she'd wash overboard. Tying her to the boat was all I could think of."

Sam squatted beside Andrew and surveyed my work. "What were you trying to do? Keel haul her?"

"What were you two doing out there in the first place?" Geoff asked.

Sam nodded. "Not the best time to confront you fear of the water, Gai."

"Oh, I'm still afraid," I said, shivering under Lori's cold stare, "but my *friend* insisted I go with her."

Everyone looked at Lori. Her golden hair clung to her pale cheeks in serpent-like tendrils. Her blue lips quivered.

Andrew peeled off his police issue rain slicker and slipped it over her shoulders. He untangled the last knot and began rubbing her ankles, encouraging the circulation to her feet. "Let's get you home, into some warm dry clothes," he said to her. "I have something to tell you."

"She already knows. In fact," I said, pointing towards the smashing waves, "that's why we were out there. She was trying to destroy evidence."

Andrew sighed. "I don't think it will matter, now. Bud's signed a confession. From here on, it's up to the court."

Lori gripped the front of Andrew's drenched shirt. "What do you mean he's signed a confession?"

He covered her hand with his own. "We really need to get you out of this weather. We'll talk about your dad, later."

Lori shook off his touch. "No. We'll talk about him now."

Andrew shrugged his wide shoulders and helped her to her feet. "If that's what you want. I went to the house to talk to your dad about Doc and your mother's relationship and before I'd asked my second question, your dad confessed to murdering Doc in a drunken fit of jealousy. Just blurted it out, like he couldn't keep it inside." Andrew tugged the edges of his coat more snugly around her. "I'm sorry, Lori. I didn't want to have to tell you like this."

"You're an idiot, Andrew MacDonald, if you believe him. He's a drunken old man who has no idea what he's talking about."

Andrew drew himself up to his full official height. Some of the gentleness was gone from his face. Sam, Geoff, me, we all pressed closer.

"Your dad had motive. Doc cuckolded him for years, sleeping with your mother. And if stealing your dad's wife wasn't enough, Doc pulled out of the golf course deal and there went your dad's retirement savings. But the last straw was Doc cheating you when he backed out of his promise to give you his medical practice. You were going to have to leave Hum Harbour. Your dad couldn't bear that so he killed Doc. I have his whisky bottle from the scene of the crime, and when the lab ever gets the DNA done it'll prove your dad was aboard the Medical Convention and switched bottles. I have witnesses that will swear Doc never touched Canadian Club. Right Gai? And I have your dad's signed confession. Case closed."

"You're saying Dad killed Doc out of love for me and planted my seaglass earring at the scene to throw you off his trail?"

He jabbed his finger at her. "You told me your pair was still in your moving boxes."

"She lied to you," I said. "Sasha and I both have our pairs. The earring on the boat has to be Lori's."

Andrew glanced from me to Lori's mutinous face.

"OK," he said to her. "You went to see Doc off and

you lost your earring on his boat. That doesn't mitigate your father's confession."

"Then why did she lie about it?" I demanded.

"She was scared. She thought it might implicate her in Doc's murder." He wiped the back of his hand across his rain soaked face. "People lie to the police all the time. Believe me, I'm used to it."

I set my hands on my hips. "OK, how about the break in at my shop, did Bud confess to that, too?"

"Not yet, but I'm sure he will."

Sam tapped Andrew's shoulder. "Uh, Andrew, little brother of mine, I, uh, don't think you'll get Bud on that one."

Andrew glanced at him. "What do you mean?"

"Well, see, I was some miffed at Gai for interfering in our lives." Sam shuffled his feet. "She's such a nosy piece of work, you know that."

I socked him in the arm.

"Well you are, Gai, face it. I'm not telling you anything you don't already know."

"So you trashed my shop?"

He held out his hands helplessly. "I was drunk. I didn't know what I was doing."

I couldn't believe it. My own brother? I fisted my hand and smacked him as hard as I could. Sam didn't even flinch. "As soon as this is over I am bringing charges against you. Just wait and see!"

Geoff cleared her throat. "Don't get too carried away, Gai. He didn't do all that damage by himself."

"What do you mean?"

Geoff inclined his head. "Do you want to explain to her, Lori, or shall I?"

All eyes were riveted on Lori and she actually smiled. You'd think she was enjoying this.

"No comment."

"Then, I will," said Geoff. "Lori went by Dunmaglass to see Gailynn. She wanted to check about Sheba. Gai hadn't called for help. Maybe she was a little curious to see how Gai was managing. After all, Gai's not known for coping well in a crisis."

I glared at him. What was this: pick on Gailynn night?

"Gai'd left her back door open. Lori went inside, but Gai was nowhere to be found."

"We'd taken Sheba to the vet in Antigonish," I said.

Geoff nodded. "Lori realized that once she found Gai's place in darkness and my car gone."

Lori pulled Andrew's coat a little tighter. "Gai was supposed to call me to help with the cat. Me, her best friend. Instead you called you." She said you with such derision my mouth fell open.

"You poisoned Sheba," I said incredulously.

Lori shrugged. "I wanted you to lay off the snooping. I know how stubborn you are but I thought a sick cat would distract you."

"So you poisoned my cat," I repeated.

Geoff said, "And busted up your shop."

I think my jaw dropped further.

Andrew inserted himself between us. "Wait a minute, here. Are you saying Lori's the one who ransacked Dunmaglass?"

Geoff nodded. "Maybe Sam broke the display cases, but Lori did the rest. When I dressed her hand after she pulled Gailynn out of the water, I realized her cuts were more than scuffs from sanding the Lori-Girl. But it wasn't until now that I put it together."

I lunged at Lori.

Geoff grabbed me around my waist and dragged me back.

Andrew stared at Lori in amazement. "You did all that to throw the scent off your dad?"

I saw Lori's face change. It was like someone had pulled down a blind inside her and my friend, my lifelong best friend, was gone. I don't think I really understood what Lori was about until that minute. I went limp against Geoff.

"It was you," I said.

Lori looked at me. Her lovely eyes were flat, contemptuous. "You've finally figured it out."

"But why?" asked Sam. "If you couldn't stand Doc, why not just let him leave town, like he planned?"

"Because he ruined my father's life. Everything my father ever loved, Douglas Campbell destroyed. Dad's marriage, his retirement, me. There was nowhere Dad could turn where he didn't see Doc's handiwork. For that, Doc had to pay."

"Doc bought you a future," I said. "You could have used your success in Halifax to take care of your dad."

Geoff understood her better than I. "The practice in Halifax would have been a constant reminder that Doc could provide for Lori better than Bud Fisher."

She shook back her wet hair. "I'd rather scrape lobster boats the rest of my life than take one penny from Douglas Campbell."

"Doc gave you life," Sam said.

Her lips pulled back in a horrible smile. "Maybe. But I took his."

35

It had been a week since Lori's arrest. I'd spent the time at home working on my jewelry, thinking, praying, crying. How did you come to terms with something as devastating as discovering your best friend is a murderer? I had no idea.

And it wasn't just Lori. My own brother had been angry enough with me to break into Dunmaglass and smash my display cases. How did I respond to that? Mom and Dad, home from that cousin's wedding in BC, wanted me to forgive Sam. It seems trashing my place was Sam's low point. Since then he'd stopped drinking, and he and Sasha were seeing Reverend Innes for marriage counseling. Mom was afraid charging Sam would sabotage the good God was bringing out of a horrible situation. I bowed to her superior wisdom all the while praying God would show me how to forgive Sam in my heart.

Not that I could rightfully claim I was above reproach in this whole affair. I had behaved abominably. Somewhere in the midst of Doc's murder investigation, I'd lost all sense of proportion. I let my hunger for justice run away with me and I broke the most basic rules of trust and human decency.

I guess it was my own sin that weighed heaviest on my heart.

Geoff had given me the week off and I used the

time to consider my options. In the end, I concluded I had only one choice.

So Friday afternoon I took my resignation to the clinic. I was close to tears because I truly loved working at the clinic. But I knew I'd broken Geoff's trust. I had no reason to expect him to want me working with him any longer.

It was four o'clock and the clinic would be closed for business. I took a deep breath, said a brief prayer for composure, and pushed open the clinic door. The place was a disaster. Kids' toys were strewn across the floor, the magazine rack overturned, and the box of tissues, usually sitting on the corner table, had been shredded by a Tasmanian orangutan—or so it looked to me.

Geoff knelt in the middle of the waiting room, collecting colored plastic blocks.

"I'm sorry but the clinic is closed for the weekend," he said without looking up. "Unless this is an emergency, I can see you when we reopen on Monday."

"Looks like you can use some help."

"Gailynn." He dropped the blocks. "Am I glad to see you." Bouncing to his feet, he rushed over and gave me a hug. "How are you doing?"

I glanced around the office, taking in the stack of unopened mail on my desk and the wobbly pile of patient folders yet to be filed. "I think better than you. Rough week?"

"Oh my gracious, yes. I'm a mess without you here." He swept his arms wide, as though embracing the whole office. "The Baxter twins."

Say no more. I set my resignation on the desk and began collecting toys, returning them to the toy box, which normally lived under the corner table, not on top of the wooden dollhouse.

"I know I gave you the week off but could you spare me enough time to help me tame this chaos?" He flashed me his most ingratiating smile. "I'll do the waiting room, here, if you'll attack the filing."

"It might be better if you did the files. You'll need to know how the system works."

He stooped to right the magazine rack. "I trust you."

I stared at his back. Trust me? Maybe I'd better hand him my resignation now.

"Geoff, we need to talk."

"Sure," he said, sliding the magazines into the rack. "What do you want to talk about?"

I passed him the envelope containing my resignation letter.

He frowned. Wiping his hands on his pant legs, he accepted the envelope, extracted the letter from within and read silently. He blew out a breath and folded the letter back into its envelope. Then he tore my resignation in half and turfed it into the crammed trashcan beside my desk. "I'm sorry, but I can't accept that."

I tugged at my hair. "You want to fire me instead?"

"No, I want you here working beside me."

"But..."

"Gailynn, we all made mistakes. What happened to Doc was terrible, and none of us will ever forget the tragedy. But there comes a point where you have to pick up and move on with your life."

"But..."

"You have to forgive yourself. I forgive you for

whatever it is you think you've done wrong. Will you forgive me?"

"Yes, but..."

"Then it's over. We solved Doc's murder. Now let's put our sleuthing days behind us and concentrate on getting to know each other better." His smile suggested some very interesting possibilities.

"Besides," he said, "what's the chance there'll ever be another murder in Hum Harbour?"

What chance indeed?

Thank you for purchasing this Harbourlight title. For other inspirational stories of Christian fiction, please visit our on-line bookstore at
www.harbourlightbooks.com.

For questions or more information, contact us at
titleadmin@harbourlightbooks.com.

Harbourlight Books
The Beacon in Christian Fiction™
www.HarbourlightBooks.com

May God's glory shine through
this inspirational work of fiction.

AMDG